Club Edinburgh Angling

Songs of the Edinburgh Angling Club

Club Edinburgh Angling

Songs of the Edinburgh Angling Club

ISBN/EAN: 9783744767989

Printed in Europe, USA, Canada, Australia, Japan

Cover: Foto ©Andreas Hilbeck / pixelio.de

More available books at **www.hansebooks.com**

SONGS

OF THE

EDINBURGH ANGLING CLUB.

Songs of the Edinburgh Angling Club

EDINBURGH
1878

SONGS

OF THE

EDINBURGH ANGLING CLUB.

WITH ILLUSTRATIONS DRAWN AND ENGRAVED
BY MEMBERS OF THE CLUB.

NEW EDITION, WITH ADDITIONS.

EDINBURGH:

PRINTED PRIVATELY FOR MEMBERS OF THE CLUB.

MDCCCLXXIX.

" We twa hae paidl't i' the burn."

" The Muse, nae poet ever fand her,
  Till by himsel' he learn'd to wander,
  Adown some trottin' burns meander,
     And no think lang ;
  Oh ! sweet, to stray and pensive ponder
     A heart-felt sang !"
BURNS.

List of Illustrations.

Engraved by William Forrest.

Preface.

N architect, when asked to furnish plans for the extension of a fine old house, is careful, if he be wise, that what he adds shall be in keeping, in design and in spirit, with the older building. He does not add Elizabethan upon Grecian, or tack some fantastic Italian wing to a grand old Scottish baronial mansion. He may not have the genius which inspired and guided the man who planned the house, and gave it dignity, and grace, and beauty; but he can have the reverential spirit which seeks to follow, even though it be at a distance, in the footsteps of his predecessor, and to do, with what skill and power he may possess, the new work which time has made unavoidable.

b

Time has made a new edition of this book necessary, not
only because the old one has been long out of print, but
because the Songs of the EDINBURGH ANGLING CLUB have
greatly increased and multiplied. The task of introducing
what is new is not easy. There must be some fear that the
new may seem scarcely worthy of the old ; and some melan-
choly reflections will intrude themselves as the pages are
turned over. Few, alas, of those who wrote and sung the
songs of old are with us now ; too many of those who have
written have since journeyed to that bourne from whence
no traveller returns, and the blanks they have left will not
easily be filled. But the work of collecting in one volume
what they did is undertaken in the spirit that, it is believed,
they would have desired. No sacrilegious finger has been put
upon the old book : it is reprinted here, from Preface
to Colophon, exactly as it was first published; and the hope
is entertained that the new volume will not be found to
be worse than the old one, simply because it is larger. The
wish which he who wrote the preface to the first edition
expressed, that the E.A.C.'s of future ages " may make better
songs and catch more fish, and prove themselves no worse
fellows on the bank and at the board " than the E.A.C.'s of
his day, has not been realised to the full. Better songs
could not well be than many of those which were written
and sung in the times which are now called of old ; but the
songs that have been written later have been conceived in the
same spirit ; and the E.A.C.'s of to-day may at least assert

that they have the same delight in the gentle art, though they may have fewer opportunities of practising it, the same keen enjoyment of their social meetings, and the same love for one another which Izaak Walton marked as the distinguishing merit of anglers, and which the older songs of the Club so justly exalt.

Since the Songs of the Club were first printed there have been changes affecting it other than those which time must of necessity bring. The "Nest" which the singers loved so much, and where they chirped so gleefully, knows the E.A.C.'s no longer. They would not willingly have left it, and, indeed, it will be seen that among the additions now made to the old volume are some which have more the character of a Lament over a great loss than of the joyous outburst of light hearts and keen wits. No one can read the songs of the past without seeing how dearly prized that "Nest" was; and Anglers being "such honest, civil, quiet men," those who loved it never dreamed that the day would come when they must bid it farewell, for they knew no cause in themselves why they should cease to be prized tenants. That day came, however—how or why it is not necessary here to re-late—and the Club had to find itself a new home. Two or three miles away,

> " Where Ashiestiel looks on the Tweed,
>   And Tweed rolls broad by Caddonlee,"

a resting-place was found; and there, a cottage, larger if not

so snug as the "Nest," was built.   It has not the honey-suckle
covered porch of the "Nest"—it is not yet shaded pleasantly
by trees as the "Nest" was; but the murmur of the
river sounds as pleasantly to its indwellers, and every
year makes the growing shade more grateful.   There, as of
old, pleasant evenings crown days well spent by the river,
and song, and jest, and cheerful conversation sweep away
the cobwebs which are apt to gather when the world is
too much with us.   Nay, if the "Medical Visitor" who
wrote what follows in the Album of the Club may be
trusted, it has potency as a sanatorium :—

A MEDICAL VISITOR'S ADVICE TO THE MEMBERS
OF THE E.A.C.

> When tired an' forfouchen,
> When hoastin' and coughin',
> When ill wi' the bile
>   Or the wee devils blue,
> Tak' your rods an' your reels,
> Throw the doctor his *peels*,
> An awa' to the Nest
>   Wi' your freins leal and true.

Beyond doubt, the writer, though professionally suicidal in
giving this opinion, was perfectly honest. His lines are at
least of as much value as most prescriptions, even with the
added mystery of medical Latin.

One difference between the newer songs of the EDINBURGH

ANGLING CLUB and those which preceded them ought to be noticed. They are less reticent about names— there is less preservation of anonymity in regard to those whose doughty deeds are celebrated. This was, indeed, inevitable. The closer and longer the association between singers and sung, the greater the familiarity and the more enjoyable the personal allusions. No attempt has been made to change or omit these; rather they have been piously preserved, because it is felt that future generations of E.A.C.'s ought to know, or have the means of knowing, who their Club forbears were, and what they did or said. The deft hand which furnished the engravings for the first volume adds others now. "Time cannot stale nor custom wither his infinite variety." Brother Forrest helps us again to make our new book bright by reproducing, with his own delicacy and appreciation, illustrations which artist members (may their shadows never be less!) have willingly contributed.

It may be permissible to say that, as of old, the Club has yet one trouble. The pollution of the waters mourned at the close of the first book still continues—nay, grows worse with ever increasing aggravation. More manufacturing villages have sprung up, and, in spite of all law and good sense, pour their poisonous refuse into the fair waters of the Tweed, to the destruction of the fairness and the fish. Let us hope that before long a change may be effected, and that those who do the mischief may be taught that they have no more right to pollute the river than they have to poison the air or set fire to the houses in their neighbourhood.

What more need be added? The new book will have a welcome from those for whom it is intended at least as warm as that which some of them and the predecessors of others gave to its predecessor. They too have had pleasure in the songs now printed for the first time, and have found them incentives to honest enjoyment by the river side. Each song has a story of its own which E.A.C.'s love to recall. No malice taints any of them: they are or were meant to be subjects for pleasant entertainment, and helps to social evenings. They were not written for show—they were written for amusement; and as they have amused E.A.C.'s in the past, it is thought that they may amuse others in the future. If they do not, a change not wholesome to contemplate will have come over the Club. That this may never be,—that as it has been in the past it may be in the future—a nursing mother of the angling muse and the gathering place of "good fellows,"—is the sincere wish of all who have taken any part in the production of this volume.

Preface

———◦———

CONSIDERING the close kinship between Contemplation and Imagination, and that Angling is the contemplative man's recreation, it is difficult to account for there being so little Angling Poetry, and for so much of that little having fallen more or less short of excellence. Nevertheless, in this respect Angling stands no lower, but much higher, than other sports. The celebration of "The Chase," it is true, has been attempted in an entire poem, which still lives, after a hundred years, perhaps not so much because it is a good poem, as because nobody has ever tried to make a better; and the same subject receives frequent allusion in other poems, and is the burden of many old and good songs. The Gun has been honoured by poets with but few and slight allusions. But Angling, although it is not the sole subject of any poem that has kept a place in litera-

ture, and is not, we have to lament and wonder, the theme
of many songs of great merit and popularity, is alluded to
by multitudes of our best poets with a frequency and affection which no other sport has been found to inspire. Still
the truth remains, that, though Angling has received many
passing honours from the Muse's hand, it has not been made
the object of such special and successful wooing as might
have been looked for from its own attractions and capabilities,
and the number and fervour of its votaries.

What may be the cause of this comparative neglect or
failure is not our business here. It may even be that there
is really no failure, except what arises from the overstrained
expectations or insatiable longings of the Angling com-
munity. True Anglers love their art so dearly, and are ever
so full of its delights, that they can never feel it to be sung
in strains sufficiently high and sweet. But be the cause what
it may, the fact, which we have a reason for here insisting
on, that Angling Poetry is generally unsatisfactory or dis-
appointing, is universally felt and admitted: just as there
is in Angling a pleasure which none but Anglers feel, there
is in the writing of Angling verses a difficulty which none
can know but those who have tried.*

Far from meaning to hint that this difficulty has been

---

* "Those who think," says Burns, "that composing a Scotch song is a
trifle, should set themselves down and try." This remark, of course, applies
to all song-writing.

overcome here, the design of this preamble is to bespeak, as a right, large indulgence for whatever defects the critic's eye may detect, or the Angler's longings feel, in the verses of this little volume. If the poets of the Edinburgh Angling Club have not proved that the gods have made them poetical as well as piscatorial, they have only failed, not merely where failure has been general, but where they did not expect nor seek success. They have written simply to please themselves, and, if it so chanced, the little knot of friends and brethren at whose request the Songs have been printed, and for whose eyes alone this book is meant; and to that amount of success they have been made heartily and thankfully welcome. By help of these verses, with their allusions to loved spots and cherished brethren, mornings by the river have seemed to smile more sweetly, evenings by the fire to pass more gleefully away,—nay, even in the dingy counting-room and buzzing court will snatches of them come o'er the mind's ear like the sweet south, till the pining "E.A.C." transports himself in soul to where he "feels the breeze down Ettrick break"; or sees the Tweed soft gliding past the Yair, or tumbling through our own "Trows"; or scents

> "The heather bell
> That blooms so rich on Neidpath Fell."

Besides the references to local scenery which form so much of the charm of these Songs to the few persons entitled or intended to be charmed, there are, as might be expected,

personal allusions, delicate or otherwise, not meant to be
universally understood, but which to those addressed suffice
to bring back the stirring incident or friendly jest which, on
some long bygone occasion, had lent added exhilaration to
the sport by the river-side, or loudness and mirthfulness to
the chirping in the "Nest."

And here it may be proper to solicit attention to the due
and becoming subordination in which the poets of the Edinburgh Angling Club have held all allusion to the subject of
indoor amusement and refreshment. This is indeed a peculiar
merit of all Angling songs. While Hunting songs almost
invariably savour more or less of the flowing bowl, Angling
songs, and especially these, are fragrant only of the flowing
stream. Not that they are of the waters watery, nor that Mr
Gough, in his present sublimated, any more than in his former
unregenerated, condition, would find himself quite at home
at Fernielee; but that Angling and the river-bank are made
the chief things,—the "Nest" and its creature-comforts only
secondary and necessary incidents. It is noticeable, more-
over, that the only allusion to refreshments partaken of
during Angling hours, is in the song of "The Saumon"
(from the pen of that true humorist and true man, the late
George Outram,—an honorary member of the Club,—whose
name, dear to all his friends, we should not perhaps thus
lightly mention); and it will be observed, both from the
narrative of the song and from its faithful illustration by the

artists, that that single exception occurred under circumstances of the greatest provocation.

It seems proper to mention, for the information of future members of the Club, as well as of an inquiring posterity, that the whole of the Songs, excepting "The Saumon," were contributed anonymously during the ten years the Club has now existed, as the production of "The Man on the Street," for the purpose of being sung at its annual festive meeting. Who the man on the street is, or was, is a mystery; for although often cited at the Market-cross of Edinburgh, and Pier and Shore of Leith, as use is, to appear at the hour of cause, he always excused himself by letter, on the score of his being, like other sons of the Muses, somewhat withered in his attire. And although it has been said that, on the evenings when the members dined together, a dingy and shadowy figure has been seen lurking near, the most generally received opinion is that, after all, the "Man on the Street" was but a myth, or a convenient name under which any member of the Club, too modest to acknowledge his poetical progeny, might "blush unseen."

Of the Illustrations, if it were necessary to speak at all, it would certainly be much worse than needless to speak in terms of apology. The only thing to be said (and it would be difficult to say it aright) is, to commend the artist-members to the special goodwill and gratitude of all the brethren, for the amount of labour, skill, and taste, of which they have made

a gift to the Club.   And, far from feeling it invidious, none
of us will more heartily than the members who furnished the
drawings accord the chief thanks and praise to Brother
Forrest, who has executed the whole of the engravings, as a
labour of love, in that style of art in which he has long stood
eminent, and in which, by the opinion of those who in such
matters speak with authority, his fame, high as it is, is far
below his merits.   And yet of the merits of these illustrations, the artistic are not the greatest in the eyes of those for
whom they are meant: every stream, and turn, and tree,
here portrayed, is to one or other endeared as the scene of
some wonderful success or dismal failure.   It was here that
A. killed the twenty-three pounder; it was there that B.
smashed his rod, and close by that C. took, not kindly nor
characteristically, to the water; it was yonder that the wor-
shipful Master of the Merchant Company, while engaged on
a benevolent mission for a brother's tackle, broke a rugged and
rapid way from the top of the tree to the bottom of the water,
to the impairing of his dignity and the destruction of those
garments of which common propriety alike requires the en-
tireness and forbids the mention.   For the sake of future
historians, it may be as well to add that none of the represen-
tations of the human form here given are actual portraits of
members, with the exception, perhaps, of the rear-view in
the illustration of "I'll awa' to Caddon," which bears a sus-
picious resemblance to a venerable member, who, on the
slightest rumour or chance of fish, small or great, is sure

thus to turn his back upon his friends and society. We must also except the figure in the illustration on page 79, which is an actual portrait drawn from the life.

Finally, this little volume is bequeathed to the "E.A.C.'s" of future ages, with the earnest hope that they may make better songs and catch more fish, and prove themselves no worse fellows on the bank and at the board, than those who in 1847 founded, and those who now, in 1858, carry on (alas! that the recollection of brethren departed should remind us of the changes between now and then) an Association whose life promises to be as long as from the beginning hitherto it has been pleasant.

Angling Songs.

The Call.

AS this book may meet the inquisitive eye of a stranger, it may be as well to explain that "The Nest," alluded to in the last verse of this Song, is the Cottage at Ferniclee, on the Tweed, occupied by the Club as their fishing quarters, and the scene of many a delightful meeting. It is called "Robin's Nest," not from that favourite of the nursery, "Cock Robin," but from its having been at one time occupied by "Robin Pringle," a younger brother of the proprietor of Ferniclee, and from its cozie, nest-like appearance. It is most faithfully depicted in the frontispiece to this volume; and certainly a more charming place is not to be found on Tweedside. No one can visit it without retaining an affectionate remembrance of its external beauty and internal comfort, or having brought to his recollection the lines of the poet—

" The river calmly swells and flows,
    The charm of this enchanted ground,
And all its various turns disclose
    Some fresher beauty varying round.

A

" The sternest heart its wish might bound,
     On earth to dwell delighted here ;
Nor could on earth a spot be found
     To Nature and to me so dear."

Not far from the Cottage stands the decayed mansion of
Fernielee. Here Miss Alison Rutherford, afterwards Mrs
Cockburn, resided, and wrote the version of the " Flowers of
the Forest, " beginning—

" I've seen the smiling of fortune beguiling."

Yair Bridge—of which a view is prefixed to the Song—
spans the Tweed in close proximity to the " Nest." Sir W.
Scott, in his review of " Salmonia," says, that in the memory of
man as many as 99 salmon (we mark the exact number) were
taken in one day at Yair Bridge ; and no one will think of
accusing the great romancer of telling a fiction. Would that
the same tale could be told now : *Sic transit*, &c. ! One could
have wished, however, that Sir Walter had told by what
means so many fish were taken. Was it with the leister,
by torchlight, or sunlight ? It must have been in the " Trows "
or " Elm-Weil " that this exploit was performed.

Precedence is given to this Song simply because it is the
first that was contributed, and the first that was sung at the
Annual Festive Meetings of the Club. It has the merit, if
it has no other, of having inspired, or at least suggested, all
the rest, save one, namely, " The Saumon." And it may
also be safely said, that had this Song not been written, the
illustrations which adorn the volume would not have been
drawn or engraved.

The Call.

TUNE—"*Jenny Jones.*"

UP, up, and away, for the winter is fled,
 With Basket and Rod let each Angler be seen ;
Now gaily the streamlet glides over its bed,
 And clad are its banks in the brightest of green.
The sweet flowers are springing on ilk sunny spot,
 The wee birds are singing on ilk budding tree ;
There's music as sweet in the reel's birring note ;—
 Then up and away to the fishing with me.

I care not for honours, I care not for gain,
    The path of ambition shall never tempt me ;
My days I would spend, free from sorrow and pain,
    Where Tweed pours its waters by sweet Fernielee.
Oh, there would I wander, from morning till night,
    With Rod and with Line the bright salmon to snare,
Then repose on its banks till the last rays of light
    Leave in shadow and stillness the old Bridge of Yair.

The delights of the chase can never compare
    With the Angler's joys as he rambles along ;
His heart, light and free as his own mountain air,
    In gladness responds to the merry brook's song.
Then up and away to the streams we love best,
    With our nice-tapered rods, and tackle so rare ;
We'll angle all day, and at night in the " Nest,"
    With toast and with song bid defiance to care.

A Bonnie Stream's the Tweed.

IT would have been an omission, in a book of Angling Songs, not to have paid a passing compliment to Mrs Phin, the oldest vender of fishing tackle in Edinburgh; and so the writer of the following Song has not been unmindful of his duty. " With PHIN's SHOP," says Christopher North, "the man who is not familiar, let him call himself not an Angler; and him will fish and trout laugh to scorn, in river and lake, in Tweed and in Loch Awe. It is a luxury to shake an angle of Mr Phin's out of the window,—fair set from butt to the topmost ring—supple as a courtier—unwarped as the principles of an honest man—ready, in its lightness, to quiver at the touch of the minnow's tongue—safe in its strength at the leap and plunge of the salmon maddening along the rapid Spey! And with what neat fingers, nice eye, cultivated taste, and sound judgment, doth his wife Margaret whip a fly! Often with the same trio have we angled a whole day, till our back bent beneath the creel, and returned them to our book, still fit for slaughter. No unpremeditated oath need ever escape the Angler's lips in the solitude who uses thy tackle; for once hooked, the tyrant of the flood is as much his property when sinking down ten fathom into a pool, or careering like a mad bull along the foamy surface, as if lying agasp on the bank, or crammed into wicker prison, himself a creelful"

Mr Phin has long since paid the debt of Nature, but his

wife Margaret still survives; and we can bear witness to the fact, that the tackle manufactured at her establishment maintains its ancient repute.

The passing allusion to "Macintosh" is well merited. The thanks of every Angler are due to the gentleman whose invention bears his name. Without Macintosh stockings what Angler, however enthusiastic, would venture into the water after 60?—With them, and a "gaucy flask" to boot, he may continue his much-loved sport, wading the waters as long as he has strength to handle a rod.

A Bonnie Stream's the Tweed.

TUNE—" *The weary pund o' tow.*"

A BONNIE stream, a bonnie stream,
　A bonnie stream's the Tweed ;
Afar frae strife I'll end my life,
　A-fishing on the Tweed.

I've coft mysel' a Rod and Line,
　Frae dainty Mrs Phin ;
A basket, and a handy gaff
　To pu' the saumon in,
　　　For a bonnie stream, &c.

I've wadin' boots o' Macintosh,
　That come aboon the knee ;
A gaucy flask is in my pouch,
　Weel charged wi' barley bree.
　　　For a bonnie stream, &c.

And in my book there's routh o' flees,
　Wi' golden winglets fine ;
Nae pages had the monks of old
　Sae beautiful as mine.
　　　For a bonnie stream, &c.

And I hae got a trusty frien',
　Wha lo'es the fishin' weel ;

Sae to the Tweed we'll jog along—
  May luck attend the creel.
    For a bonnie stream, &c.

Then bring the Rod, the Reel, the Gaff,
  A merry time we'll lead ;
And lengthen out the pirn o' life
  A-fishing on the Tweed.
    For a bonnie stream, a bonnie stream,
      A bonnie stream's the Tweed ;
     Afar frae strife I'll end my life,
      A-fishing on the Tweed.

The Capture.

TUNE—" *The Monks of old.*"

AWAY, away, to the stream, brave boys!
　　The rain has pelted all night;
The river is running from bank to brae,
　　Hurra! for the sparklers bright!

But soon shall its foaming rage subside,
　　And the fish see the blue sky again;
But it's pleasanter far, when the water's brown,
　　To show them the grass-green plain.

Hurra! hurra! here's the river's edge!
  Now brandish the rod on high;
Away goes the line, like an arrow straight,
  Like a snow-flake falls the fly.

A dash! a plash! the good fish bites,
  Then hies for the stormy deeps;
But a turn of the wrist and the hook is fast—
  Halloo! how he tumbles and leaps!

Give him line! give him line! away he runs,
  While merrily dances the reel;
Thou ne'er yet belied me, my good tough rod—
  Be faithful thou trusty steel.

He slackens—he falters—wind up! wind up!
  Now gently guide him to land;
A feeble flap of his fine broad tail,
  And he gasps on the yellow sand.

Come, gie's a Sang.

TUNE--"*Tullochgorum.*"

"COME, gie's a sang!" our Preses cried,
"For ance I wunna be denied;
This nicht let care be laid aside,
    And a' the gloomy quorum.
In fishin', jokin', we delight,
Fishin', jokin', fishin', jokin',
In fishin', jokin', we delight,
    And Walton we adore him;
In fishin', jokin', we delight,
And we resolve again to fight
Our battles o'er, withouten spite,
    To the tune o' 'Tullochgorum.'

"The rain is meltin' doun the snaw,
The frost is drappin' fast awa',
Our hearts are saft'nin' wi' the thaw,
    A-thinking o' Salmorum.*
We'll catch them, souple tho' they be,
Catch them souple, catch them souple;
We'll catch them, souple tho' they be,
    And then we'll quaff a jorum.

* If it be objected by some nice critics that "Salmorum" is not good Latin, we admit the fact; but assert that it is good rhyme, which is of more consequence.

We'll catch them, souple tho' they be,
Before they scamper to the sea,
Then boast the sma'ness o' the flee,
    To the tune o' 'Tullochgorum.'

" Now fair fa' him where'er he be,
O' th' Angling Guild a Brither free,
May he ne'er want his barley-bree,
    And saumon, a great store o' 'em.
We'll toast him bravely, four times four,
Toast him bravely, toast him bravely ;
We'll toast him bravely, four times four,
    Wi' hip, hip, variorum ;
We'll toast him bravely, four times four,
And wish him blessings many a score,
While every Angler cries *encore*,
    To the tune o' 'Tullochgorum.'

" For him who ca's an Angler fool,
The Angling-rod a silly tool,
We hae nae heart to wish that dool
    And sorrow may come o'er 'im ;
But ever empty be his flask,
Ever empty, ever empty ;
But ever empty be his flask,
    And saumon ne'er afore 'im ;
But ever empty be his flask,
And barley-bree ne'er scent his cask ;
And we'll sing dumb if he should ask
    The song o' 'Tullochgorum.' "

The Merry Angler.

Tune—" *The Merry Sunshine.*"

I LOVE the merry, merry Angler's life,
  He leads a life so gay,
As by the brook he wanders
  Each day is a holiday.
In all that breathes around him,
  From bird, and flower, and tree,
A heavenly beauty haunts him,—
  Oh! the Angler's life for me!
      The Angler's life, the Angler's life,
        The Angler's life for me;
      The Angler's life, the Angler's life,
        The Angler's life for me!

I love the merry, merry Angler's life,
  Afar from haunts of men,
Where the only din's the waterfall
  As it tumbles down the glen;
And the only salutation
  Is the trout that leaps so free,
As to kiss my fly it boundeth,—
  Oh! the Angler's life for me!
      The Angler's life, the Angler's life, &c.

I love the merry, merry Angler's life,
 When day has sunk to rest,
And brothers of the Angle meet,
 To show whose creel is best :
Oh ! then what merry tales we tell,
 What pleasant songs we sing !
And the ready laugh and chorus
 Make roof and rafters ring.
   The Angler's life, the Angler's life,
   The Angler's life for me ;
   The Angler's life, the Angler's life,
   The Angler's life for me !

The Reveille

OF THE

Edinburgh Angling Club.

TUNE—"*All the blue bonnets are over the border.*"

UP! up! lads o' the rod and reel,
  Mornin's the time for sport on the border;
Haste! haste! for Neidpath and Elm-Weil,
  The Boat Pool o' Yair, and the Trows are in order.

The mist's awa' creepin', the salmon are leapin',
  The brown Hills o' Yair the sun is adornin',
The south wind blows fine now, for casting your line now,
  Then up to your fishin', lads! up in the mornin'.
    Up! up! lads o' the rod and reel, &c.

Nane o' your sleepy heads, jump frae your drowsy beds,
  On wi' your fishin' claes,—sloth be your scornin';
If you for sport incline, in the Trows cast your line,
  Sure o' a saumon this fine fishin' mornin!
    Up! up! lads o' the rod and reel, &c.

Haste wi' your rods and reels, bring out your clips and creels,
  Bring out your saumon flees all in good order;
On wi' your wadin' boots, ne'er think o' fishin' trouts,
  Saumon's the sport to enjoy on the border.
    Then up! up! lads o' the rod and reel, &c.

I'll awa' to Caddon.

" CADDON," celebrated in the following Song, is a small stream which flows into the Tweed, at Caddonlea, about a mile below Ashiestiel, long the abode of Sir Walter Scott. In his *Minstrelsy of the Scottish Border* he informs us that the scene of the affray at "Katharine Janfarie's" bridal is said, by old people, to have been upon the banks of the Caddon, near to where it joins the Tweed.   The stream is thus alluded to in the old ballad which bears the name of "Katharine Janfarie" in the *Minstrelsy* :—

> " The blood ran doun by Caddon bank,
>   And doun by Caddon brae,
>   And sighing, said the bonnie bride—
>   ' O wae's me for foul play !' "

Caddon flows through a pastoral valley; and from its source to its junction with the Tweed, presents a picture of quiet beauty which cannot fail to delight the eye and heart of every lover of Nature, especially the Angler.   It is the haunt of many a disciple of the gentle craft, more particularly of a much-esteemed and honest piscatory friend, who has set much of his affections on it, and who is supposed to celebrate its charms in the following verses.

The allusion to the "perturbed" and "unperturbed" in the last stanza will be understood by many Members of the Club.

I'll awa' to Caddon.

TUNE—"*Sally in our Alley.*"

SOME boast the Tay, and some the Clyde,
    And some the Tweed are mad on ;
For nane o' them care I a fig,
    Sae I'll awa' to Caddon ;
For Caddon is the wale o' streams,
    As frae the hills it rushes,
Then gently murmurs o'er its course,
    Or jinks amang the bushes

I've fished the Leader, and the Lyne,
    The Armit, and the Talla ;
My heart leaps up when I think on
    The days I've spent on Gala ;
In Luggit, too, I've cast my flee,
    And many a fish have had on ;
But tho' these streams are dear to me,
    They ne'er can match wi' Caddon.

No hideous rocks disturb its course,
    O'er pebbles bright it's strayin',
It's ripple is like music sweet,
    As round a scaur it's playin';
Its banks are green, its pools are deep,
    And swarm wi' fish sae bonnie,
Oh ! tell na me o' ither streams,
    It is the best o' ony.

So fair a scene will bring repose
    To him that's aye perturbed,
Or gently stir the soul of him
    Whom nothing ere disturbed.
Then cheer your heart, each Angler dear,
    Nor worldly things look sad on ;
But mount your basket and your rod,
    And aff wi' me to Caddon.

The Parson's Pool.

THIS Song was suggested by the following incident :—The author and a friend were fishing for salmon in the Ruel (a stream which flows through Glendaruel in Argyleshire), near to the Manse of ——, when a lad bawled out, " You're no' to fish that pool ; it's the Minister's." The author passed on, obedient to the injunction, by no means desirous of having a quarrel with the Parish Minister ; but his friend lagged behind, and when he next made his appearance he had captured a fine grilse. He did not admit that it was the produce of the " Parson's Pool." Grave suspicions, however, were expressed to the contrary ; and the joke was considered too good to be lost, and not unfit to be preserved in rhyme.

It appears to have been not unusual for " the Minister," whose Manse had the good fortune to be situated near a fishing stream, to reserve a pool for himself. On the Slitrig, at Hawick, and near to where the old Manse stood, there is a pool still known as the " Minister's Pool," and where, we have no doubt, many a goodly fish was caught in days of yore. But alas ! the pool is now sadly defiled with dye-stuffs and other pollutions, to the destruction of all animal life ; and thus one of the most beautiful objects in Nature—a running stream —is rendered an eye-sore and a nuisance. Should not an offence like this be made criminal ?

The Parson's Pool.

TUNE—"*The Soldier's Joy.*"

WOULD you wish to know
Where your angle to throw?
 Try the Parson's Pool, the Parson's Pool;
For the Parson, I'm told,
Like the monks of old,
 Ne'er wants a goodly fish in his Pool.

The Pool is deep,
And the Salmon leap,
 In the morning cool, the morning cool;
If you're anything sly,
There cast your fly,
 You're sure of a fish in the Parson's Pool.

As I took my way,
In the dawning gray,
 By the Parson's Pool, the Parson's Pool:
"You've no permission,"
Cried a lad, " there to fish in;
 Don't fish, if you please, in the Parson's Pool."

But the moment he turned
The advice I spurned,
 Of the Parson's fool, the Parson's fool;
And when no one was nigh,
I dropt my fly,
 And caught a fine fish in the Parson's Pool.

A Right Merry Garland,

TO BE SUNG BY

Each Jolly Angler of
The Edinburgh Angling Club.

LET them talk of their clubs literáry,
　　With their black-letter tomes wondrous rare ;
Of their clubs where they meet to get mellow,
　　Where there's smoking and drinking to spare.

Let them doat on their curling and bowling,
　　And their clubs for all sorts of games ;
On their clubs for the good of the nation,
　　We pause not to reckon their names.

But of all their fine clubs you can mention,
　　Whether learning or sport bears the rubs,
There's none can compare with our " Angling,"
　　Our " Angling's " the King of the Clubs.

Let the black-letter clubs print their volumes,
　　Which no one cares ever to read ;
Let other clubs sigh o'er their jorums
　　For a glimpse of the bright rolling Tweed.

As for us, while the river flows onward,
　　And rain-clouds bedarken the sky,

We'll covet our health in our pleasure,
And cherish the rod and the fly.

So here's to each jolly Waltonian,
May he never adversity feel ;
And while he can handle his tackle,
May he never want fish in his creel.

The Departure.

TUNE—" There's nae luck about the house."

GUIDWIFE, gae fetch my fishing gear,
    The wading boots, the creel,
The whisky-flask, the book o' flees,
    The gaff, the rod, and reel.
        For I maun hae a day on Tweed,—
          Aye, maybe I'll hae twa ;
        The music o' the birring reel
          Has charms for fishers a'.

Stay, stay, guidman, a word on that;
  I dinna like that Tweed,—
It's fu o' crukes, and rocks, and holes,
  That yet may be your deid.
            Sae dinna think upon the Tweed,
              Oh! dinna gang awa';
            Tho' weel I ken the birring reel
              Has charms for fishers a'.

Wheest, wheest, guidwife, I've gane fu' aft,
  And ne'er gat skaith, ye ken;
But brought ye aften hame a fish,
  To grace your table en'.
            Sae I maun hae, &c.

Ye wadna' hae your ain guidman
  Toil on frae day to day,
And see these locks ye aft hae praised
  Turn prematurely gray.
            Sae I maun hae, &c.

I fished the Tweed for mony a day
  Before I ca'd ye mine;
And mony a fish, wi' tackle guid,
  I've tane in Tweed since syne.
            Sae I maun hae, &c.

And mony a fish I hope to kill,
  While I can throw a flee:
Sae up, guidwife, mak' haste, and bring
  My fishin' gear to me.
            For I maun hae, &c.

There's something true in what ye say,
  Sae I withdraw my plea;
And here's your fishin'-traps and gear,
  And flask o' barley bree.
      For ye maun hae a day on Tweed,—
        Aye maybe ye'll tak' twa;
      For weel I ken the birring reel
        Has charms for fishers a'.

But tho' I yield, it's my advice,
  O' a' Tweed's deeps tak' care;
O' rocky Neidpath, and the Trows,
  And Burnet's Cairn, beware!
      For ye maun hae, &c.

And hear ye, mind to change your claes,
  Ilk steek should ye get wat;
Then tak' a dram, and rin nae risks,
  Great luck, and haste ye back.
      Agreed, guidwife! for I maun hae
        A day, aye maybe twa;
      The music o' the birring reel
        Has charms for fishers a'.

The Return.

TUNE—"*Guid forgie me for leein'.*"

YE'RE back frae the fishin', and welcome, guidman ;
But why are you lookin' sae droll, man ?
Oh ! dear pity me, ye ha'e riven your breeks,
And the uppers frae aff your shae-sole, man—shae-sole, man !
 The uppers frae aff your shae-sole, man !

Oh ! losh guide us, Willie, there's nocht in the creel,
Far better ye never had gane, man ;
Was there thunner aboon, or was Tweed in a flood ?
Or the fish, were they lookin' for rain, man—for rain, man ?
 Or the fish, were they lookin' for rain, man ?

But I see thro' it a', ye intend a bit trick,—
Ye hae left them out yonder to kipper ;
That's mindfu' eneugh, for a bit noo and then
Is fu' tasty for breakfast or supper, or supper,
 Is fu' tasty for breakfast or supper.

Guidwife, haud your tongue ! ane's no aye in luck,
As sometimes I ken to my sorrow ;
Tweed's swarming wi' fish,—it's rather owre big,
But it will be in fettle to-morrow, to-morrow,
 It will be in fettle to-morrow.

Dinna speak o' gaun back,—be contentit at hame,--
Gang to market wi' me for ilk fin, O !
The siller-hook's sure to catch better by far,
And's cheaper than roe, flee, or minnow, or minnow,
 And's cheaper than roe, flee, or minnow.

Ye Anglers of Edina.

Tune—" Ye Mariners of England."

Ye Anglers of Edina,
Who fish the silver Tweed,
Whose rods have o'er its waters waved,
Where circling eddies speed ;
Your lines and flies prepare again,
To catch the finny foe,
As ye sweep o'er the deep,
While the gentle breezes blow,—
While the trout are leaping fresh and strong,
And the gentle breezes blow.

A trout as big's a salmon
Shall start from ev'ry wave,
Then strike for Walton and for fame,
Nor dread a wat'ry grave ;
Where your Captain leads the van,
Your tackle lightly throw,
And sweep o'er the deep,
While the gentle breezes blow,—
While the trout are leaping fresh and strong,
And the gentle breezes blow.

The Angler fears no hardships,
Of care he does not dream,

His march is o'er the rippling wave,
His home is on the stream ;
With the magic of his wand above
He charms the fish below,
As they pour round the shore,
When the gentle breezes blow,—
When the trout are leaping fresh and strong,
And the gentle breezes blow.

The reel's delightful music
Shall sound on every burn,
Till Spring and Autumn both are past,
And the Winter chill return ;
Then, then, ye jolly Anglers,
The toast and song shall flow
To the fame of his name,
Who kill'd the noblest foe,—
While the trout were leaping fresh and strong,
And the gentle breeze did blow.

I Lobe to go an-Angling.

TUNE—"*Charlie is my darling.*"

I LOVE to go an-Angling,
  An-Angling, an-Angling,
I love to go an-Angling,
  And fish frae year to year.

'Tis when the rain has ceas'd at last,
  The stream's becoming clear,
And noisy brooks are brawling past
  I' the Autumn o' the year,
    I love to go an-Angling, &c.

And if I hook a salmon fine,
  Tho' he should break away,
I book him certain to be mine
  Upon another day.
    And thus I go an-Angling, &c.

But if I have him in my creel,
  Be this my heart'ning true,—
The stream's in tide—the flee is leal—
  And I am sure of two.
    And thus I go an-Angling, &c.

The Angler toils,—no salmon leaps !
  But who hears *him* complain ?
He's tranquil as the river deeps,
  When clearing after rain.
    And thus he goes an-Angling, &c.

A Weel-Filled Creel.

"TAMMIE SCOTT," alluded to in the following Song, was the host of a well-known house of entertainment and resting-place for the Angler at Clovenford. Neither Tammie nor his wife was a model innkeeper, and came in the end to be their own chief customers ; but both are now gone to parts unknown,— Tammie being dead, and his wife being known to have followed him,—at least as far as Glasgow.

Clovenford is pleasantly situated on the banks of the Caddon, about a mile above its junction with the Tweed, and is thus noticed by Wordsworth in his *Yarrow Unvisited :*—

> "From Stirling Castle we had seen
>   The mazy Forth unravelled ;
> Had trod the banks of Clyde and Tay,
>   And with the Tweed had travelled ;
> And when we came to Clovenford,
>   Then said my 'winsome marrow,'
> Whate'er betide, we'll turn aside,
>   And see the braes of Yarrow."

Every reader, too, of Professor Wilson's delightful articles upon Angling, titled "Anglimania," will be familiar with Clovenford, and the different localities on the Tweed in its neighbourhood.

A Weel-filled Creel.

TUNE—"*When the kye come hame.*"

COME all ye jolly Anglers,
  Who handle rod and line,
Leave aff your merry tales awee,
  And push aside the wine ;
I'll tell you o' a pleasure,
  Which none but Anglers feel,—
'Tis returnin' frae the water
  Wi' a weel-filled creel.

A weel-filled creel,
A weel-filled creel ;
'Tis returnin' frae the water
Wi' a weel-filled creel.

What signifies to boast and blaw
   O' this fish and o' that,
The muckle ane that brak' the line,
   The nibbles that we gat ;
" The big ane—sure 'twas twenty pun', "
   He kent its weight fu' weel ;
Gie me the proof that nocht can ding
   A weel-filled creel.
         A weel-filled creel, &c.

See yonder pawkie carle,
   Wi' laughter in his e'e,
He has nae time to tak' his glass,
   Or crack a joke wi' me ;
Sae eager to be at the sport,
   He bolts wi' rod and reel,
And smilingly frae Caddon brings
   A weel-filled creel.
         A weel-filled creel, &c.

When Spring comes in, arrayed wi' smiles,
   And flowers bedeck the lea ;
When vernal breezes round us blaw,
   And fill the heart wi' glee ;
The Lawyer, and the Painter too,
   Will aff to Tweedside steal,

Desertin' desks and easels for
   A weel-filled creel.
      A weel-filled creel, &c.

Should care oppress the Angler's heart,
   And a' things look agee,
Just leave the noisy toun awhile,
   And jog along wi' me.
Ae day beside Tweed's siller stream
   Will drive care to the deil,
And send you hame rejoicin' wi'
   A weel-filled creel.
      A weel-filled creel, &c.

And when you're wearied out at nicht
   Wi' flourishin' your wan',
A tiresome gate 'twixt you and hame,
   Nae "Tammie Scott's" at han';
Ye'll ha'e the satisfaction
   It's no wi' yill you reel,
But merely stachrin' wi' the load—
   A weel-filled creel.
      A weel-filled creel, &c.

Then leeze me on the Angler's haunts,
   There I would spend ilk day,
'Mang mossy glens and solitudes,
   Where burnies wimplin' stray ;
And then at e'en, 'neath cozy bield,
   I'd toast a' fishers leal ;
And may their sairest burden be
   A weel-filled creel.—A weel-filled creel, &c.

E

Oh! where do Anglers Hide their Heads?

[Imitated from Haynes Bayley's ballad of "Oh! where do Fairies hide their heads?"]

OH! where do Anglers hide their heads
  When snow lies on the hills;
When frost has closed the river-beds,
  And hushed are all the rills?
Farewell the rod, the reel, the gaff,
  Adieu the grassy plain;
No Angling pleasures can they quaff,
  Till green leaves come again.
    Till green leaves come again,
      Till green leaves come again;
    No Angling pleasures can they quaff,
    Till green leaves come again.

Perhaps in Law's tempestuous court,
  'Mid streams of talk they stray;
While silly clients are their sport,
  Entangled day by day.
Perhaps in some sly, cozy nook
  Their ardour they maintain,
By telling o'er the fish they took,
  Till green leaves come again.
    Till green leaves come again, &c.

When they return, then will the brooks
  With music fill the air ;
And fishing-rods, and lines, and hooks,
  Be busy everywhere.
The salmon, to escape the lure,
  Will try his arts in vain ;
And every Angler fill his creel
  When green leaves come again.
    When green leaves come again,
      When green leaves come again ;
    And every Angler fill his creel,
      When green leaves come again.

The Disappointed Angler.

THE incident which suggested the two following songs occurred in the autumn of 1851. The day had proved very
unpropitious, not a fish having been killed, although several
rods had been busy on the water from an early hour of
the morning. The party at the "Nest" had finished their
second jug after dinner, and the gloamin'—that witching hour
for anglers as well as lovers—was fast coming on, when one
of the party resolved to have another cast in the "Trows"—a
favourite pool or succession of pools—before the sun went down.
Near the foot of the "Trows," at a place called the "Brander,"
a large fish, after the second or third throw, rose to the fly, but
missed it. Although the cast was repeated several times, the
fish would not stir again, and darkness ultimately drove our
angler from the river, but not before he had resolved on another trial after he and the fish had had a night's rest. The
fact of a fish having shown itself in the "Brander" could not be
concealed from the rest of the party. Our angler reached
the "Trows" next morning by six o'clock, having driven from
Clovenford, where he was residing, a distance of nearly three
miles; but he was just in time to see his anticipated prey
stretched on the rocks by the skilful hand of a brother Angler,
whose "earlier flee" had wiled the "scaly buffer" from the
depths of the "Brander." The temper of even a less enthusiastic fisher might have been ruffled by the disappointment,
but he bore it with his accustomed equanimity. The fish
weighed 14 lbs., and was in excellent condition.

The Disappointed Angler.

TUNE—"*The Lass o' Gowrie.*"

" 'TWAS on a summer afternoon,
    A wee before the sun gaed doun,"
That to the "Trows" I wandered doun,
    In hopes to catch a saumon;
I threw my line across the stream,
    Which glittered in the evening beam,
When to my fly, wi' sudden gleam,
    Arose a sonsy saumon.

I started back wi' strange delight,
    For, oh! it was a wondrous sight;
Its size so big—it shone so bright—
    It was a dainty saumon.
I fished it o'er and o'er again,
    Till back and arms did ache wi' pain;
But no! it wadna come again,
    The stupid, senseless saumon!

The day had faded in the west,
    So hame I trudged to tak' my rest,
Nor stopt to pree aught at the "Nest"—
    Resolved to pree that saumon.
But first I marked where it did lie,
    Then upwards gazing at the sky,
I vowed next morn that it should die,
    If ever died a saumon.

I dreamt a' nicht 'bout rod and reel,
    My book o' flees, my fishin'-creel,
An otter, too, that cam' to steal
    Awa' my bonnie saumon.
The sun had tinged the eastern sky,
    When frae my bed, light as a fly,
I rose, my skill again to try,
    And catch that wily saumon.

I reached the "Trows," but oh, the shock!
    My heart beat quick, my knees did knock,
For clots o' blood lay on that rock,
    The blood o' my poor saumon.

Noo, Anglers a', be warn'd by me,
    When next a fish you chance to see,
Tell not a frien', whae'er he be,
    Keep your secret and your saumon.

*The following is another version of the same incident,
by a different hand :—*

The Beauty o' the Stream.

Tune—"*Jock o' Hazeldean.*"

" Why wait ye by the tide, laddie ?
    Why wait ye by the tide ?
'Tis surely time to seek your hame,
    And meet your bonnie bride ;
And meet your bonnie bride, laddie,
    That's bricht as sunny gleam."
But aye he vowed he'd wait awee,
    For the beauty o' the stream.

" Now lay this Angling keen aside,
    Put up your rod and reel,
When next to-morrow's dawn you greet,
    That fish may bite your steel.
Oh ! if your skill you still must try,
    Await a kindlier beam."
At last he vowed he'd come again
    For the beauty o' the stream.

Next morn the stream rolls in its pride,
　The Angler keen is there,
And eager hearts are side by side,
　The coming sport to share.
Alas! the fish in vain they seek,
　It's vanished like a dream:
Another's earlier fly has caught
　The beauty o' the stream!

The Mist Leaves the Hill.

Tune—" They may rail at this life."

THE mist leaves the hill, and the south wind blows soft,
The "Trows" and the "Elm-Weil" are swarming with fish ;
Then up, brothers, up, your rods flourish aloft
Where Tweed flows as lovely as Angler can wish.
To the heart of yon deep pool away goes the fly,—
There's a plunge, and the rod now is bent like a bow ;
How he rushes and leaps !—'tis in vain—he must die ;
Bring the gaff, bring the gaff, in his pride he'll lie low.

Nay, he's off !—like a dart through the water he goes !
Oh ! be true, my good fly, and flow freely, my line !
Now slowly he swims to the place where he rose ;
But vain are his wiles, for he soon shall be mine.
Yes, he yields !—and as gently as ever a child
Was led by its mother, he comes to the land ;
He turns on his side, to his fate reconciled,
Hurra ! boys, hurra ! he is stretched on the strand !

F

A Lament.

THE following attempt at an imitation of "The flowers of
the Forest" was hastily jotted down one afternoon iu the
"Nest," while the other members present were "chirping"
over their cups, and was suggested by the beggarly account
of empty baskets which the records of the Club sometimes
bear witness to, giving countenance to an opinion, that in a
few years the salmon would become

"A thing to dream of, not to see."

It is to be hoped, however, that the recent legislation for the
more effectual preservation and increase of salmon in the
Tweed, notwithstanding the many shortcomings in the Act,
will by-and-by turn the lamentation of the Angler into joy.

This is the only song in which the " Man on the Street " has
ventured to allude personally to any of the members of the
Club.   The Committee of Editors, upon whom the pleasant
duty of editing the Songs was devolved, at first thought of
omitting the names of the members alluded to ; but on further consideration they judged it better to allow them to remain, and they have little doubt that the individuals whose
names are here imperishably recorded will pardon the liberty
which has been taken with them.

It is scarcely necessary to add that the song is to be read
not as a picture of a state of things already in existence,
but as foreshadowing what was likely to happen.

A Lament.

Tune "*The Flowers of the Forest.*"

THERE'S nae fishin' noo, lass,
   I'll ne'er be missin' noo, lass,
Ye'll ne'er noo be wauken'd before break o' day ;
   Nae leistrin', nae boatin',
   The rod it lies a-rottin',
Since Tweed's silver beauties are a' wede away !

I've seen the time in,

Known nowhere noo but rhyme in,

When saumon-reel gaed birrin' like spinnin'-wheel for aye ;

But noo a' is still as

The leaves upon the willows,

With no breath to stir them upon an Autumn day.

Forrest stays at hame, noo,

Russel grows quite tame, too,

E'en Morton's content to relinquish his prey ;

They count it uncommon

To look for a saumon

Since Tweed's silver beauties are a' wede away !

The " Nest " 's noo deserted,

The Club's broken-hearted,

Wi' a' their gear they've parted that saumon used to slay ;

They're wand'rin' thro' the streets, noo,

Like men who've lost their wits, noo,

For Tweed's silver beauties are a' wede away !

The Angler's Winter Song.

TUNE—" *The Old Folks at Home.*"

ICE, ice, upon each flowing river,
    Where I would stray !
My sad heart is longing ever
    For the warm, sunny ray.
Oh, I dwell with animation,
    On blythe days gone,
When, in Angling recreation,
    I never felt alone.

CHORUS.
    Oh, this frost is cold and dreary,
        Ev'rywhere I roam !
    O, Anglers ! how, my heart grows weary
        For the river with its foam !

Fishes, queer must be your feeling,
    Poor, prisoned slaves !
Peering at that icy ceiling,
    From your dark, rocky caves.
Do you break your heads in leaping,
    Trying a rise ?
Or spend your lone hours sleeping,
    Dreaming fondly of flies ?

CHORUS.

Oh, this frost is cold and dreary,
    Ev'rywhere I roam !
O, Anglers ! how my heart grows weary
    For the river with its foam !

But a brighter time is coming
    For you and me,
When the glad bee shall be humming,
    On the gay, flowery lea ;
And the reel join in merry chorus
    With the brook's song,
While the lithe rod is whistling o'er us,
    Cheerily all day long.

CHORUS.

Still the frost is cold and dreary,
    Ev'rywhere I roam ;
O, Anglers ! how my heart grows weary
    For the river with its foam !

The Angler's Spring Song.

TUNE—" *The Bush aboon Traquair.*"

WHENE'ER the frost begins to thaw,
   I'm lively as a lintie ;
When ice and snaw melt fast awa',
   O' fishin' I've a glintie ;
And so, tho' a' the Winter through
   I've been sae dou and eerie,
I feel the Spring within my veins,
   And wow I'm wondrous cheerie.

I first tak' doun my limber rod,
   And screw it up fu' tightly,
Then poise the wan' wi' steady han',
   And throw it out sae lightly ;
And thinkin' I hae hooked a fish,
   I gie a sudden wap, sir ;
But oh ! my han's been out o' use,
   And I hae broke my tap, sir.

Next I tak' up my buik o' flees,
   And turnin' o'er its pages,
Each weel-kent wing fresh visions bring
   O' byepast golden ages.

'Twas this ane kill'd the muckle trout,
   This ane that grilse sae braw, man ;
'Twas this ane tempted frae its hauld
   That monarch o' a saumon.

Then I live thro' the youthfu' days,
   When wi' an Angling brither,
We wandered o'er the heathy moor,
   And fish'd the loch thegither ;
Nor parted till the settin' sun
   Gaed doun behint the mountain,
And frae the torrent cam' the wail
   O' the spirit o' the fountain.

Then come awa', my trusty frien',
   Your tackle a' be sortin' ;
Hae rod and line, and ilk thing fine,
   For now's the time for sportin' :
Your " winsome marrow " leave awhile ;
   The lowe o' love's aye burnin'
Mair bricht, when to your ain fireside
   Frae fishin' ye're returnin'.

The Saumon.

TUNE—"*The Angels' Whisper.*"

ON Tweed side a-standin',
　　With long rods our hands in,
In great hopes o' landin' a Saumon were we ;
　　I took up my station,
　　With much exultation,
While Morton fell a-fishin' farther doun upon the lea.

G

Across the stream flowin'
My line I fell a-throwin',
A sou'-wester blowin' right into my e'e ;
I jumpt when my hook on
I felt something pookin' ;
But upon farther lookin', it proved to be—a tree.

Deep, deep, the stream in,
I saw his sides a-gleamin',
The king o' the Saumon, sae pleasantly lay he ;
I thought he was sleepin',
But upon farther peepin',
I saw by his teeth he was lauchin' at me.

The flask frae my pocket
I poured into the socket,
For I was provokit unto the last degree :
And to my way o' thinkin',
There's naething for't but drinkin',
When a Saumon lies winkin' and lauchin' at me.

There's a bend in the Tweed, ere
It mingles with the Leader,
Perchance you may see there a wide, o'erspreadin' tree ;
That's a part o' the river
That I'll revisit never ;
'Twas there that Scaly Buffer lay lauchin' at me.

Let us go to " Robin's Nest."

TUNE—" *Kelvin Grove.*"

LET us go to "Robin's Nest," brother Anglers, O !
From worldly cares to rest, brother Anglers, O !
> There we'll throw the tempting fly,
> Where Tweed runs rushing by,
And the wary salmon lie, brother Anglers, O !

Oh ! to quit the dinsome town, brother Anglers, O !
All that makes us fret and frown, brother Anglers, O !
> To the Tweed let us repair,
> And if fish we don't ensnare,
We shall breathe the caller air, brother Anglers, O !

Each pool shall share our love, brother Anglers, O !
Their treasures we shall prove, brother Anglers, O !
> The Trows, and Neidpath too,
> The Elm-Weil always true,
Yield enjoyment ever new, brother Anglers, O !

And when our sport is o'er, brother Anglers, O !
What talk we'll have in store, brother Anglers, O
> Fernielee, the Brig o' Yair,
> Tweed's banks that bloom sae fair,
And the deeds we hae done there, brother Anglers, O !

Then haste to "Robin's Nest," brother Anglers, O !
From worldly cares to rest, brother Anglers, O !
> There we'll throw the tempting fly,
> Where Tweed runs rushing by,
And the wary salmon lie, brother Anglers, O

The Champion.

THIS song is intended (though not very successfully, the Author admits) to commemorate the capture of a large salmon by R——— C———, one of the members of the Club, on the 5th of November 1855, the day before the river closed for the season.   The event caused no small sensation among the other members who were present, and who had unsuccessfully plied their rods all day.   If we are not mistaken, it was the only fish killed on the occasion.   It weighed 20 lbs., and was in all respects a beautiful fish.   The scene of the exploit was a pool or stream known as "Arres' Put," one of the most delightful spots on the river, and a favourite place with most Anglers : many a goodly fish has been drawn from its depths.   In the season of 1856 another member of the Club hooked and played a fish in this pool for four hours,— not by Shrewsbury clock, but by his own patent chronometer,—and had the ill-luck to lose it (that is, the fish) in the end.   The weight of the lost fish was of course enormous ; because, as invariably happens, it is the largest fish that escape.

The Champion.

TUNE—"*Le Petit Tambour.*"

COME fill your glasses high ;
   A bumper toast I claim
To him that killed the noblest fish—
   The " Champion " be his name.

It was a gallant fish, my boys—
   A giant of its race—
By nature formed, let all confess,
   A monarch's board to grace.
      Then fill your glasses high, &c.

Full twenty pounds it weighed, my boys ;
   Its match ne'er left the sea ;
A sight it was to charm the eye,
   And fill the heart with glee.
      Then fill your glasses high, &c.

Light as the dew-drop fell the fly,
   Where the flashing waters sweep ;
When from his lair, like lion bold,
   He saw the salmon leap.
      Then fill your glasses high, &c.

As bends the mast before the storm,
   When seas are raging high ;

So did this salmon bend the rod,
When first it seized the fly.
Then fill your glasses high,·&c.

Oh ! how its broad tail lashed the wave,
While the reel went merrily round !
Yair's " sister heights "* caught up the notes,
And echoed back the sound.
Then fill your glasses high, &c.

Long, long the contest lasted, boys !
It was a glorious sight ;
But *science* vanquished every wile,
And victory crowned the fight.
Then fill your glasses high, &c.

Its panting sides like silver shone,
As on the bank it lay ;
With loud huzzas the welkin rung
To the hero of the day.
Then fill your glasses high, &c.

Long be that hero famed, my boys !
The prince of Anglers he ;
And when he next a-fishing goes,
May we be there to see.
Then fill your glasses high, &c.

---

*   .   .   .   " Russet bare
Are now the sister heights of Yair."
MARMION.

The Invitation.

TUNE –" *The Weaver's March.*"

NOW Spring comes in wi' mirth and glee,
    And lichts wi' joy each Angler's e'e;
Then tak' your rod and gang wi' me,
    To fish the Tweed sae bonnie.

The heath-cock crows on Neidpath Fell,
The cowslip blooms in Caddon Dell;
And Nature, wi' her magic spell,
    Mak's a' things blythe and cheerie.

Then gang wi' me to Ferniclee,
The sweetest spot on Tweed to me ;
But sweeter far when shared wi' thee,
    My ain, my trusty crony.

We'll wile the saumon frae its lair,
Where gently flows the stream by Yair,
Wi' tackle fine, and flees as rare
    As e'er glanced on the water.

Or else upon his haunts we'll steal,
Where pine trees shade dark Elm-Weil,
And echo mocks the birring reel,
    Sae welcome wi' its music.

And when the sun sets in the west,
And sends the Angler to his rest,
We'll seek within the " Robin's Nest "
    Those joys which never weary.

Sir Walter Scott, in communicating to Mr Robert Cham-
bers his personal recollections of Mrs Cockburn, the authoress
of " The Flowers of the Forest," says :—"A turret in the
old house of Ferniclee is still shown as the place where the
poem was written." The illustration at the head of this song
is a view of a portion of the old house with the turret referred
to. It is fast hastening to decay.

The Sun glints over Neidpath Fell.

It is scarcely necessary to remark, that "The Forest," alluded to in the following song, has no reference to an accomplished Angler—a member of the Club—who handles his burin with as much skill and dexterity as he handles his rod, as the engraved illustrations which adorn this book amply testify. "The Forest gray" is Ettrick Forest, once the hunting-ground of the monarchs of Scotland, and one of the most picturesquely beautiful districts in the south of Scotland.

"Neidpath Fell" is part of the shooting-ground rented by the Club; it is a hill of considerable dimensions rising behind the "Nest," and is thus alluded to in *Marmion* :—

> "Away hath passed the heather-bell
> That bloom'd so rich on Neidpath Fell."

Immediately in front of the "Nest," with the Tweed flowing between, lies the district of country, with its sombre hills, known as Ettrick Forest. Ashiestiel, too, which will for ever remain associated with the name of Scott, is close at hand; so that altogether the locality is one not only of beauty, but of surpassing interest. Many a basket has been filled with beautiful trout from a stream which "winds by Ashiestiel,"

H

and many a goodly salmon has there yielded to the prowess of a veteran Angler and kind-hearted man—alas! now no more. Mr Turnbull of Peel (a farm adjacent to Ashiestiel), the person alluded to, was an honorary member of the Club.

The Sun glints over Neidpath Fell.

TUNE—"*The Miller of Dee.*"

THE sun glints over Neidpath Fell,
  And lights the Forest gray;
The dew-draps glisten on the grass,
  The cock proclaims the day.
Then up, my lads ! cast care aside,
  Throw business to the de'il;
We'll fill our baskets frae yon stream
  That winds by Ashiestiel.

Let ithers toil frae day to day,
  This warld's gear to win,
Or seek in pleasure's vain pursuit
  For joys they ne'er can fin';
But gie to me my weel-worn creel,
  My ain rod in my han'
And tho' I'm poor, I envy not
  The noblest in the lan'.

What tho' my locks are lyart grown,
  And age has dimm'd my e'e,
Wi' steady aim and skilfu' han'
  I yet can throw a flee.

The Angler's heart can ne'er grow auld,
   Or aught o' grief retain :
Ance mair beside the sunny stream,
   And he is young again.

When head and han' are tired alike
   Wi' wark that kens nae rest ;
When care sits cowrin' on the heart,
   And life has lost its zest ;
The balmy breeze upon my cheek,
   The gowan on the lea,
The saft sough o' the limber rod,
   Aye gladness bring to me.

And oh ! to see the trouties leap,
   In a' their speckled pride ;
A silly, senseless fool is he
   Wha would our sport deride.
Then up, my lads ! cast care aside,
   Throw business to the de'il ;
We'll fill our baskets frac yon stream
   That winds by Ashiestiel.

The Angler's Delights.

Tune—"*Tullochgorum.*"

WHEN Skinner wrote his famous sang,
    Wi' praises loud the kintra rang;
Roun' mony a cheerie hearth fu' lang,
    'Twas sung wi' mirth an' glee, man;
But this that I'm about to raise,
Belangs to fame since Walton's days,
And stirs the heart-strings wi' its lays,
    Till glam'rie comes wi' speed, man;

For o' their tunes I wat fu' weel,
There's nane can match the birrin' reel,
When trout or salmon bite your steel,
    Frae aff the Banks o' Tweed, man.

What pleasure is there sae divine
As fishin' wi' the rod and line,
Awa' frae care your griefs to tine,
    At bonnie Fernielee, man?
There's pleasure sortin' o' your flees;
There's pleasure in the balmy breeze;
There's joy to see the salmon seize
    Your flee upon the stream, man;
There's hope renewed in every cast;
There's rapture when we hook him fast;
And breathless ardour when at last
    We haul him to the shore, man.

When fishers meet awa' frae hame,
There's music in their ev'ry theme;
There's music in the very name
    O' fishin'-rods and lines, man;
Then let us aff wi' a' our glee,
To fish the Tweed at Fernielee;
For that's the spot where we agree
    To spend our leisure time, man;
To fish wi' minnow, bait, or fly,
And a' the Angler's slicht to try,
And slock our drouth when we are dry,
    In " Robin's Nest " at e'en, man.

"𝔇um 𝔠apimus 𝔠apimur."

Life is like a running stream,
      Heigh ho !
Darking now, and now a gleam,
On its banks we sit and dream,
      Heigh ho !

Still the stream is running on,
      Heigh ho !
Soft o'er moss, now rough o'er stone,
Mirthful now, and now a moan,
      Heigh ho !

Anglers all, we're fishing there,
      Heigh ho !
Catching trifles light as air,
Till death takes us unaware,
      Heigh ho !

Vox Piscis.

It is not the first time that strange revelations have come from the bellies of fish. We do not refer to our nursery tales merely; nor need our friends be told that, if stones can preach, fish may tell tales; and that, if "books in the running brooks" are to be found, fish are the most likely to fall in with them, and to digest them, too. That three treatises found in the belly of a cod gave rise to a tract, entitled "Vox Piscis, or, the Book Fish," should be well known to all readers of Halieutics; and we may remind them of the parallel story of "a shark, who having swallowed the log-book of a vessel that had been scuttled after the massacre of the crew, and afterwards repenting, took the first hook that offered, and turned king's evidence, so as to hang the villains, from the revelations made by the documents in its inside" (*Badham's Fish Tattle*). After these instances, our piscatory friends will not wonder that such "fish tattle" as is narrated in the following verses should have occurred at a real fish-dinner party, and that the incident it commemorates should turn out to be as truthful as many after-dinner colloquies among Anglers, when the fish are made to come off second best. In truth, the *jeu d'esprit* is founded on fact; and we are sure no one will enjoy its pleasantry more than the gentleman whose mishap called forth the *Vox Piscis*.

Vox Piscis:

A NEW ANGLING BALLAD.

TUNE—"*The Laird o' Cockpen.*"

An auld-farrant group o' fish i' the Tweed
Aince met in Neidpath Pool to feed,
In the month o' June, ae beautifu' day,
When nae Angler was near to cause dismay.

And after dinner they had their chat :
Some talk'd o' this, and some o' that ;
But the merriest tale that day was tauld
Was this, by a saumon wary and auld :—

" An Angler cam' to the river side,
    I saw him frae under the rowin' tide ;
    A comical figure I trow was he,
    Tho' he fancied himself o' nae sma' degree.

" Wi' his basket and gaff across his back,
    His wadin' boots, without flaw or crack,
    His rod o'er his shouther he carried sae gran',
    He thocht him an Angling Gentleman.

" As hidden I lay beside a gray stane,
    On a sudden a thocht cam' into my brain :
    This Angling hero wha comes to destroy
    Us puir silly fish, I'll try to decoy.

I

" And so when he throws that monstrous thing
  That he ca's a ' fly,' with its hideous wing,
  I'll mak' a pretence to catch the fly,
  Then adieu to the sport o' this fisher sae sly.

" He jerket his fly across the stream,
  But a' was peace, like a Quaker's dream ;
  He threw again, and a stealthy rise,
  Made him think he had seized the glitterin' prize.

" Again he threw, on slaughter intent,
  But o'erbalanced, into the deep water he went ;
  He was droukit ; his boots were fu' to the brim ;
  And fishin' that day was nae mair for him."

W Forrest Del. et Sculp.

Angling Fancies.

DEDICATED TO THE SHADE OF THE LATE T. HAYNES BAYLEY.

TUNE—"*I'd be a Butterfly.*"

I'D be an Angler, born near a river,
    Nightly its murmurs would lull me asleep;
Daily its banks I'd be roving for ever,
    Enticing the bright ones that gleam in the deep.
I'd never care for city-bred pleasures,
    Seeking for mine where the gentle waves leap:
I'd be an Angler, watching my treasures,—
    The sportive and bright ones that gleam in the deep.

My magical wand would be gift of a fairy,
   Her's, too, my hooks with their beautiful wings ;
And she'd spin me a line of that stuff light and airy,
   That over her bower the gossamer flings.
Oh! then for the trout so watchful and wary!
    Each summer's day's ramble a basketful brings :
I'd be an Angler in league with a fairy,
    And lodge in a bower where the sweet linnet sings.

But were this denied me, and each finny rover
   Were shy as a maiden when lovers draw near,
Surely 'tis better, ere life's dream is over,
   To Angle in hope, tho' hope disappear.
Oh! Winter will come, and too soon discover
    That Angling, like life, must draw to a close ;
But who would not Angle on, just like a lover,
    And heed not the thorn when in view of the rose ?

The Joyous Angler.

TUNE—"'*Twas within a Mile of Edinburgh.*"

THE Tweed's but a glint frae Edinburgh toun,
　And the buds begin to appear ;
The Angler has ta'en his fishin'-rod doun,
　For he yearns for the sport that's near.
Come, my lassie, I'll away ;
　You won't say your laddie nay ;
But to his coaxing she would say,—
　　　No, no, it can't be so ;
　　　　I cannot, cannot,
　　　　Wonnot, wonnot,
　　　　Mannot let thee go.

Sandy was a lad buckl'd to his desk,
　The feck o' the days i' the year ;
Contented he toil'd at his ilka-day task,
　But he felt the tear and the wear.
And tho' still sae blythe and gay,
　Angling was his prop and stay ;
So to his wife he'd gently say,—
　　　Yes, yes, it shall be so ;
　　　　You cannot, cannot,
　　　　Wonnot, wonnot,
　　　　Mannot say me no.

Sandy is gane to the bonnie, bonnie Tweed,
 The art he so well lov'd to ply ;
It was joyous to look on the lusty trout,
 As they sprung at his tempting fly.
And as he fish'd sae blythe and gay,
 And aroun' his hook they play,
The finny beauties seem to say,—
   Ho ! ho ! it must be so ;
    We cannot, cannot,
    Mannot, mannot,
    But in his basket go.

𝔄ngling 𝔄dbentures.

THE incidents attempted to be versified in this song are not apocryphal, but occurred somewhere on the Tweed, though not at Neidpath, the assigned locality.

The story of the toothless fish is this :—The Captain alluded to in the song was fishing one day with a young friend, a novice in the art of Angling. However, sometimes the worst Anglers catch the most fish,—a reflection with which an accomplished Angler, we are told, is pleased occasionally to console himself. It chanced on this occasion that the Captain's friend, after a few throws, and before the Captain had stirred a fin, hooked a fine fish, which, after sundry directions from his mentor, the young Angler succeeded in landing. It proved to be a goodly 10-pounder. The Captain eyed the fish for a little, and then evidently chagrined at his friend's success, he threw it on the ground with an air of intense disgust, exclaiming, "The brute has no teeth !" It is said, notwithstanding, that the fish had as good a set of teeth as ever adorned the mouth of a salmon. Still, that a greater *lusus naturæ* than a toothless salmon may exist, no one will doubt who believes the following description from Fletcher's Play of *A Wife for a Month*—

" I'll tell you more : there was a fish taken,—
A monstrous fish, with a sword by's side—a long sword—
A pike in's neck, and a gun in's nose—a huge gun—
And letters of mark in's mouth from the Duke of Florence.
    Cleanthes.   This is a monstrous lie."

We are disposed to agree with Cleanthes; but the fact alluded to in the song of a salmon having, after a desperate struggle, sprained the Captain's wrist, is no fiction ; and if any one doubts it, we can only say with Richard Franck, " Let him angle for Anchovies." And who, some one may ask, was Richard Franck? He, too, was a Captain, and fought under Oliver Cromwell ; but " when wild war's deadly blast was blawn," he doffed his corslet and steel cap, assumed the rod and the basket, and made an Angling tour through Scotland, as far as Sutherlandshire,—an account of which he afterwards published in his " Northern Memoirs suited for the Meridian of Scotland." We can easily fancy Chantrey in his studio, surrounded by beautiful objects of his own creation, and Chantrey by the river side busy with his Angle ; but it requires an effort of the imagination to figure one of old Noll's troopers—who fought possibly at Naseby or Worcester —transformed into a peaceful Angler, and discoursing on the quiet beauties of Nature, and the delights of the contemplative man's recreation; yet Franck's book is full of such discourses, and he shows himself to have been a true sportsman and skil- ful Angler, both for trout and salmon. Still, the contrast may not be more striking than between Nelson pacing the deck of the " Victory " in the heat of the fight, and Nelson quietly fishing in the Wandle, at Merton ; for, as is well known, Nelson was an Angler.

It was a frequent boast of the Captain of the song that the lines which he used were spun from the silken locks of many a fair lady. Besides their attractiveness to strange and capricious, and it might be sentimental, fish, he said that the oil which the hair had imbibed rendered them impervious to water, and consequently as light and airy after a day's fishing as at its commencement : hence the allusion in the song.

It was never our good fortune to see the Captain handle a rod or cast a line, far less hook, play, and land a 20-pound " saumon,"—the very perfection of human skill,—but we are told by competent judges that he was no indifferent Angler. He was, however, slow to do justice to the merits of his brethren of the craft ; and we know that on one occasion he designated an expert and skilful Angler, once a member of the Club, " a coarse fisher," although all—even an " unconcerned spectator "—who have seen him handle a rod or play a fish will acknowledge that few Anglers could do the one or the other in a more masterly way.

K

Angling Adbentures.

TUNE—" *The Boatie Rows.*"

I coost my line in Neidpath Pool,
    And hook'd a salmon strong ;
He hied him to the stony deeps,
    And there he struggled long.
        A merry time, a merry time,
           We honest Anglers lead ;
           And blythsome are the days we spend,
             When fishing on the Tweed.

A Captain brave stood by my side,
    And well he counselled me ;
And when I did that salmon kill,
    " He has no teeth !" said he.

The Captain tried his skilful hand,
    With line of purest hair,
Spun from the silken ringlets of
    Edina's darling fair.

At last he hook'd a mighty fish,
    Long, long it did resist,—
" He's off ! he's off ! alas !" he cried,
    " But oh ! he's sprained my wrist."

Yet still the Captain angled on,
   Intent a fish to slay ;
But not another fin was stirred
   On that eventful day.

But many a funny tale was told,
   And many a harmless jest,
Till Sol behind the wild Minchmoor*
   Had sunk to take his rest.

And when in pensive mood I stray,
   I cannot choose but wish,
Some friend the riddle would unfold
   Of this strange, toothless fish.

To charm the eye, and please the taste,
   A finer fish ne'er left
Old ocean's depths to cleave the flood,
   And be of life bereft.

A thing of beauty, it is said,
   Will prove a joy for ever ;
So while I live this toothless fish
   Forget it shall I never.
      Oh ! a merry time, a merry time, &c.

---

* *Minchmoor* is a high hill separating Tweeddale from Ettrick Forest. Across it is a bridle road to Selkirk ; and it was by this mountain-path that Montrose fled from the battle of Philiphaugh. From the top of Birkendale Brae, a steep descent on the south side of Minchmoor, we have the first view of the woods of Hangingshaw, the Castle of Newark, and the romantic dale of Yarrow.

Why Wreath the Sword?

Why wreath the sword with myrtle?
　In rust let it be laid;
Behold the havoc it has caused,
　Behold the blood-stained blade!
To home-felt joys pay honour,
　Give them the myrtle wreath;
But, oh! allow the cruel sword
　To rest within its sheath.

No crown to jolly Bacchus
　Let beauteous woman weave,
His frenzied joys are sorrows,—
　They glow but to deceive,
But wreath with glorious myrtle
　The Angler's loved abode,
And hang—an arch above his door—
　The peaceful Angling Rod!

The Tweed.

TUNE—"*Afton Water.*"

I'LL sing of the Tweed, as it rolls to the sea,
From Tweedshaws to Berwick, bright, sparkling, and free,
Through morass and muir, through valley and lea,—
I'll sing of the Tweed, as it rolls to the sea.

I'll sing of the Tweed, the lovely, the fair,—
For where is the stream with the Tweed can compare?
Go search all broad Scotland, south, north, east, and west,
The boast still shall be—of all streams it's the best!

Let others discourse of the smooth-winding Tay,
Or tell of the charms of the swift-rolling Spey,
Of the Dee and the Don, the Forth and the Clyde;
But I love the fair Tweed as a bridegroom his bride.

It gathers its tribute from many a rill
Leaping joyous and pure from the far distant hill,
Where the heath-cock, and plover, and lone curlew dwell,
And the grouse builds its nest 'neath the sweet heather-bell.

From its rise 'mid the hills to its home in the sea,
There is not a spot but is cherished by me;
The Minstrel's loved theme—while romance with its spell
Invests every ruin, and haunts every dell.

How gently it murmurs by Castle and Ha',
By Manor and Cottage, and green waving shaw !
Or where the old Abbey, so stately and grey,
Is woo'd by its·song as it rolls on its way.

Flow on, queen of rivers ! by Cottage and Bower ;
We sport on thy banks for one brief sunny hour,
And muse as thy waters sweep tranquilly on
The same at this hour as in ages long gone ;

So in ages to come, as in those that are past,
The hum of thy music shall rise on the blast ;
And on thy green banks the blythe Angler shall stray,
And mix with thy notes the glad strains of his lay.

Conclusion.

IN the song entitled "The Return," printed at page 26 of this volume, "Willie's" "winsome marrow" winds up the domestic colloquy by advising her husband, who has returned from an unsuccessful salmon fishing, not to go back again, but to remain contented at home, and go with her in future to the market, as being a cheaper and surer mode of catching fish. This may be called the economic, and prosaic minds will think it the common-sense, view of the matter.

There is no doubt that salmon-fishing, while it is the most exciting and fascinating, is also the most uncertain and unproductive department of Angling ; and as putting the question on its proper footing, we think we cannot do better than print the following passage from an article contributed to the *Quarterly Review* for January 1857, by the same member of the Club who has furnished the Preface which introduces this volume. Besides the appropriateness of the passage selected, it is worthy of a more permanent place than the ephemeral pages of a Review ; while the allusion to the "happenin' beast" and the "transient brute" localises a description which many members of the Club will recognise, and gives prominence to a functionary of the Club,—who will at once be detected by the "portrait'" at the top of the preceding page, which, though the artist has taken his subject in the rear, is a striking likeness.

"But *is* the salmon good for sport ? There actually are people who will ask such a question, though to many others it seems to verge on the insane, if not on the profane. Perhaps there may even be some who, after being assured that the salmon *is* good for sport, are capable of asking next, what is *sport* good for ? But to this extreme class we merely reply that it is good for health and for amusement—at least as good for those purposes as much of the walking and riding that is done under the sun, and greatly better than most of the eating, drinking, and dancing that is done under the chandelier. We may consent to admit—for it is nothing to the purpose—that salmon-angling is actually one of the most costly, and is apparently—that is, to the eye of all but the person suffering—one of the dreariest and most desperate of recreations. The expense and the labour are great ; the recompense is inappreciable, and often quite invisible. The average cost of a salmon taken on the rod-fisheries of the Tweed (and Tweed is not an extreme case) varies between £3 and £5 (the market-value, taking all kinds and sizes together, being perhaps about 4s. on the average), counting nothing for time and for travelling expenses : the latter item, it must be understood, being proportionately very heavy ; because a salmon-fisher cannot, like a grouse-shooter, remain at his station for weeks together, but is restricted to only two or three days after each flood. Yet the money is cheerfully paid, and the disappointments no less cheerfully endured. Salmon-fishing is indeed a passion, perhaps unaccountable as to its origin, but certainly irrepressible in an ever-increasing proportion of the people ; while in individuals, the appetite once implanted almost invariably grows rapidly to the end on the very little indeed that it now-a-days has to feed upon. It is strange to think of the exceeding desperateness of the chances of success which now suffice to tempt men away from their business and their families to some of our salmon-streams ; yet those who have most often felt and seen the hopelessness of the undertaking are just those who are most eager to try it again. Look at that otherwise sensible and respectable person, standing midway in the gelid Tweed (it is early spring or latest autumn, now the only seasons when there is a chance), his shoulders aching, his teeth chattering, his coat-tails afloat, his basket empty. A few hours ago, probably he left a comfortable home, pressing business, waiting clients, and a dinner engagement. On arriving at his 'water,' the keeper—as the tone of keepers now is—despondingly informed him that there is 'nae head (shoal) o' fish,' although

L

at the utmost 'there may be a happenin' beast'; or, as we have heard it expressed, with that tendency to a mixture of Latinism with the Border *patois* which is to be ascribed, we suppose, to the influence of the parochial schools, 'There's aiblins a transient brute.'   But in his eagerness and ignorance he knows better than the keeper; and there he is at it still, in his seventh hour.   The wind is in his eye, the water is in his boots; but Hope, the charmer, lingers in his heart. To many this is a marvel, considerably greater than that which Byron stated and explained :—

'Though sluggards deem it but an idle chase,
   And marvel men should quit their easy chair,
   The toilsome way, and long, long league to trace,
   Oh! there is sweetness in the mountain-air,
   And life that bloated ease can never hope to share.'

For surely it is still more marvellous that men should quit not only their easy chairs, but their native and proper element, in pursuit of something which they very seldom obtain, and which is to be got at home for a twentieth part of the money and no trouble at all.   Yet many there be that commit this folly, and find a sufficient reward.   'And pray,' asks the objector, 'what is *that?*'   Obviously something which unbelievers are incapable of understanding and unworthy of enjoying.   It has been maintained, though not perhaps in cool print, by men of sense and sobriety—men not ignorant of any of the delights which flesh has served itself heir to—that the thrill of joy, fear, and surprise (now-a-days surprise is the predominating emotion) induced by the first *tug* of a Salmon, is the most exquisite sensation of which this mortal frame is susceptible—whether he comes as the summer grilse, with a flash and a splash ; or, like a new-run but more sober-minded adult, with a dignified and determined dive; or, like a brown-coated old inhabitant, with a long pull, and a strong pull, low down in the depths.   Without discussing this point in all its aspects, moral and physical, it is enough that, for a very small chance of attaining the Salmon-Angler's delight, whatever it is, there are multitudes prepared to pay and suffer, without asking anything whatever that is injurious to other men or to the public weal.   Nor is it to the purpose that there are moments—rather, perhaps, only one moment—when the angler himself may half suspect his own rationality: the moment when, after having toiled all day and caught nothing, he turns, soaked and shivering, to the hut which is his home for the night, seeing in his mind's eye his disapproving wife, his unanswered letters, and especially his vacant chair at the board of the friend whose good opinion and better dinner he has recklessly forfeited.   For a moment the inclination seizes him to say with Touchstone in the forest, ' When I was at home I was in a better place.'   But it is but for a moment, and then follows another strange effect.   How is it that on or near the river-side everything he sees or tastes seems better than are better things at better places ?—bad whisky better than the best claret, braxy mutton than the choice of Leadenhall, the conversation of a decidedly unintellectual keeper or boatman than the best *mots* of the best got-up diner-out, and the repose on the pallet of chaff or straw deeper and sweeter than often visit beds of hair or down.   Come how it may, come it does, that the discussions, the jokes, the incidents of times like these, the memory cherishes and chuckles over through many years, and especially through many dreary 'close-times,' when multitudes of things, doubtless much brighter and less worthy to fade, have been forgotten, or are remembered but as wearinesses? 'In short, the whole affair,' concludes the objector, 'even on your own showing, does not stand to reason;' an idea which perhaps indignant Anglers would prefer to express by saying that reason does not stand to it."

We cannot resist transplanting from the same quarter other two passages; the one relating to the perils to which the salmon is exposed in its marine wanderings, and the other to a question interesting not only to Anglers, but to every lover of the beautiful in Nature :—

"In the spring of 1852, about 500 kelts were marked with gutta-percha rings, duly numbered, in a pool, within a few yards of tide-reach, at the bottom of the river Whitadder, which joins the Tweed immediately above Berwick. The circumstances were somewhat unfavourable, a long drought retarding the departure of the fish, but doubtless the great majority of them got safely away. And they went away for ever. None returned, and only three of them were ever heard of, in each case under circumstances of the most distressing character. One of them was caught at the mouth of the Tyne, 70 miles to the south; another at Yarmouth, 300 miles to the south; and the third at Eyemouth, 10 miles to the north, the last individual being found in the stomach of a cod, with nothing remaining of him but his vertebral column and his gutta-percha ticket. These simple but certain facts convey a painful and pathetic idea of the remoteness and the perils of the salmon's marine wanderings. Compassion and indignation mingle at the idea of a fish of high family, gentle-manners, and fastidious taste, leaving for ever the sweet-flow-ing Whitadder, to compete with base-born bloaters at Yar-mouth, or find an inglorious grave in the maw of a vulgar Scottish cod :—

'Ah, little did thy mother think,
   That day she cradled thee,
What lands ye were to travel round,
   What death ye were to dee !'

From such facts we draw only one 'practical improvement,' as the Scottish clergy term the best and briefest part of their discourses—that the fact of such great multitudes perishing, when beyond our help, in the wide and wicked sea, is, though not exactly an encouragement, an additional reason why we should take the better care of them during the periods when they are our wards and guests."

*　　　*　　　*　　　*　　　*

" There is a question even greater than the Salmon ques-tion, and which cannot too soon receive the most solicitous attention of the public. That question is not, Shall we pre-serve our fish ? but *Shall we preserve our rivers* ? The increased and ever increasing size of our inland towns, and the great though but yet commencing change in domestic arrangements and the system of town-drainage, are raising the unpleasant question whether it is necessary or endurable that all the rivers of the country should be transformed into common sewers. The evil is but beginning—at least in such regions as those intersected by the Tweed ; but it is growing rapidly, and is by its nature difficult, if not impossible, to arrest, ex-

cept in its beginnings. Hitherto our large towns have been
chiefly—in Scotland entirely—on the coast or within tide-
reach on some estuary or navigable river, and their drainage
has gone off to the sea with comparatively little harm or offence, except in such extreme cases as London and perhaps
Glasgow. But now the railway system, with its cheap and
rapid carriage of materials, goods, and fuel, is enabling manufacturing towns to rise in far inland localities; and the
fact is gradually appearing that such towns, sending their
drainage for scores of miles down the rivers, do, or at least
will, create a really national nuisance—a nuisance greater
than that produced by towns many times their size situated
within the cleansing influences of the sea-tide. The woollen
manufacturers on the banks of the Tweed and its tributaries
now make almost no use of the wool produced on the hills
overhanging their own tall chimneys, but bring their materials from Saxony and Australia, their coals from the Lo-
thians and Northumberland, and find their markets over all
the world : what has been done there can, and we hope will, be
done in other inland districts; and we rejoice to see Hawick,
Selkirk, and Galashiels already on their way to be Brad-
fords and Halifaxes. But contemplate the results of having
large towns fifty or sixty miles from the sea, with contribu-
tions from every village and even farmhouse, sending their
whole refuse down the river channel through four counties !
Look at what the Tweed is now, in contrast with what will
be its look and smell at that not distant *then.* See her and
hers rolling along, beautiful and beautifying, through regions
where every ruin is history and every glen is song, gathering
her tributes from a thousand hills—from where sweet Teviot
sings unceasingly its ' Farewell to Cheviot's mountains blue ;'

where pensive Yarrow winds like a silver, chain amid 'the dowie dens;' where, in the sad and silent 'Forest,'—

'The wildered Ettrick wanders by,
    Loud murmuring to the careless moon,'—

till, grown stately, massive, and brimming, 'Tweed's fair river, broad and deep,' wheeling beneath the donjon keep of Norham and the battlements of Berwick, sinks into the ocean as glittering pure as when she broke away from her native hills. Is all this to vanish, and in its place a pestilential sewer? Is that which now spreads health and beauty around to become an eyesore extending over half the breadth of Scotland? Shall the turrets of Abbotsford be reflected from a monster gutter, all stains and stench? Shall fair Melrose, instead of being 'viewed aright by the pale moonlight,' be nosed in the dark? Forbid it, all the powers of Parliament? If, indeed, that prohibition could not be uttered without destroying or impeding the brisk and cheerful industry which has sprung up among those sweet hills, there might be nothing for it but to sigh and submit. But it would be almost profane to doubt that from so great an evil there must be means of escape—that Hawick may prosper and yet Tweed be preserved. The manufacturers in great towns have already been made to consume their smoke, and the time seems coming when compulsion to the same effect will be aplied even to London householders—when even 'the sacred domestic hearth' shall be invaded by the officers of Sanitaryism. The Londoners are at present seeking for some means of subjecting themselves to a prohibition of continuing to make a sewer of their own Thames; and can it be doubted

that when the people of the towns on the Tweed and other
such rivers shall find or be made to find the *will*, there will
be comparatively little difficulty about the *way* to prevent
them making an ignoble and pernicious use of a river which
is *not* their own, but is the property of four counties and the
pride of Two Kingdoms."

Additional Songs.

My First Salmon.

TUNE—"*Alley Croker.*"

WHEN late I gaed to live on Tweed,
    To spend a month's vacation,
I buit to share in what is there
    The common recreation—
Sae I bought a rod, wi' brass weel shod,
    The height o' Peebles steeple,
And bulky books o' braw busk'd hooks
    That stunn'd the Tweeddale people.

For fishing gear I didna spare—
    Creel, boots, and gaff, an a', man ;
For I had keenly set my heart
    On naething less than saumon.

I threshed a week through stream and crock,
    Till I was fairly scunner'd ;
For fient a fin I e'er brought in,
    And wife and bairnies wunner'd.
The neebors roun', and wags frae toun,
    In mockery lamented ;
And poachers sly, as they passed by,
    Glower'd at me as dementit—
While I, with keen and eager look,
    Sae eident and sae slaw, man,
Endeavour'd wi' my patent hook
    To wile out my first saumon.

I thocht, indeed, o' leavin' Tweed,—
    I couldna thole sic scornin'—
Till frae my bed, by instinct led,
    I banged up ae gray mornin',
Resolved ance mair the stream to dare,
    When nane would be observin' ;
For the evil eye o' passers by
    My fingers aye kept swervin' ;
And doun would thud my ravell'd snood,
    Creating sic a jaw, man,
That little prospect ere had I
    O' ought but fleying saumon.

When I gaed out, cam' fear and doubt ;
   For o'er the water porin',
Twa Tweeddale clods, wi' roosty rods,
   The streams were sly explorin'.
They look'd on me wi' scornfu' e'e,
   As ane wi' little gumption,
But wha intent on sic a scent,
   Show'd plenty o' presumption ;
For wha, they mutter'd, ever heard
   O sic a want of awe, man,
As for a fisher ae week auld
   To dream o' catchin' saumon !

Guid luck, at last, gae me a cast—
   My stars they now were brightnin'—
My light-thrown snood scarce touch'd the flood,
   When down it flew like lightnin'.
My heart resiled, my een grew wild,
   The landscape round gaed whirlin',
But quick as light I wauken'd bright
   To my pirn wildly skirlin',—
Which noo I held to like a helm,
   And sae tentily did thraw, man,
That I had noo a nearer view
   O' grippin' my first saumon.

The Tweeddale louns—they heard the souns,
   And saw the fierce contention ;
Sae doun they ran to lend a han',
   Wi' traitorous pretension.

I cried, " Haud aff ! let go the gaff !"—
    And, spite o' their persuasion,
I spurn'd their help, for now I felt
    I rose to the occasion ;
Sae giving line, and feeling fine,
    I let. him gently draw, man ;
And when he took a sulky fit,
    I tickled my first saumon.

How can I tell a' that befel—
    I fish'd like inspiration ;
And mason lads frae dykes in squads,
    Look'd on wi' approbation.
Frae neebor hills ran shepherd chiels,
    Wi' collies mad careerin',
And cheer'd like wud, while by the flood
    The Tweeddale louns stood jeerin' ;
Hoping, aye expecting, keen,
    That something might befa', man,
That yet a novice might deprive
    O' grippin' his first saumon.

At last, cleek'd fair wi' canny care,
    In silver sheen sae splendid,
A saumon sound, o' thirty pound,
    Lay on the bank extended ;
Nae tasteless dish o' " lyin' fish,"
    But ane run fresh frae ocean ;
The first that year in Peeblesshire—
    Was ever sic commotion !

Sae fresh was he run frae the sea,
    The lice stood in a raw, man,
And laced like beads the gaucy sides
    O' this my sonsie saumon.

The news flew aff like telegraph,
    And reach'd the toun before me ;
And auld and young their wark doun flung,
    To stare at and adore me;
My eldest loun, wi' parritch spoon,
    Half naked ran to meet me,
While at the door, wi' smiles in store,
    My guidwife stood to greet me,—
Protestin' loud before the crowd,
    That she ne'er heard or saw, man,
O' sic a monster of the deep
    As this, the gudeman's saumon.

" What wad ye wish done wi' this fish ?"
    My wife began inquirin'—
" The minister maun hae a share,
    His kindness is untirin'."
Sae down it went, and up was sent
    A dinner invitation—
Then to a party saumon-pang'd,
    I gave a lang narration
Of how I fought, and how I wrought,
    And still held by the maw, man,
This leviathan o' the Tweed,
    My first—and my last—saumon.

Now, far and wide through a' Tweedside,
   I'm look'd on as perfection ;
In manse and ha' I crousely craw,—
   I've form'd a wide connection.
The *Scotsman*, scann'd through a' the land,
   Announced the feat astoundin' ;
Then in the *Field* it was reveal'd,
   And in *Bell's Life in London*—
A' tellin' o' an Em'bro chiel,
   A sportsman fresh and raw, man,
Who had such luck, and show'd such pluck,
   In grippin' his first saumon.

Angler's Reveille.

TUNE—"*Fill the Bumper Fair*"—(*Moore's Melodies*).

WHA wad stay in toun,
　　Wha to business settle ?
Tweed's been roarin' doun,
　　And noo's in famous fettle.
Shoals were seen to press
　　By Kelso Brig on Sunday—
Travelling express
　　For the Nest on Monday.

Then fill the flask wi' speed,
　　And store the cigar casket,
And cram wi' beef and bread
　　The largest fishing-basket.
And should guidwife be out,
　　Orra bits o' pickin'
Seize, as lawfu' loot,
　　Ham, cold pie, and chicken.

Now hail a cab, and drive
　　Like fury, to the station,
Where clubmen fast arrive,
　　In joyous exultation.
How the jolly crew
　　Gratulate each other,
With a loud halloo,
　　And whacks upon the shouther !

N

The engine, proud to bear
   These glorious sons o' Walton,
Impatient snorts to tear
   Her way right through the Calton.
Now she speeds to Tweed,
   Spurning Portobello,
Spieling up Tynehead,
   Twisting doun the Gala.

At the loud guffaws
   Which from our carriage thunder,
Turnip-howers pause,
   Wi' gaping mouths o' wonder.
Stationmasters dour,
   Stand the anglers' chaffing,
And have scarce the power
   To ring their bells for laughing.

Now safe at Galashiels
   We light our weeds—then pad on,
Breastin' o'er the hills
   Bounded by the Caddon.
Now by Fernielee,
   Wi' lengthened steps descending,
The cottage smoke we see,
   O'er the Tweed impending.

Robert, at the door,
   Impatient for his callans,
Hails the joyous corps
   In hamely Scottish Lallans.

But noo we must address
　　Ourselves to the unpacking,
That at our evening mess
　　Nae comfort may be lacking.

What a varied feast !
　　And a' thing in profusion—
Though on the table placed
　　Wi' something o' confusion.
A board so rarely crowned
　　An epicure might tickle,
For friendly boxes round
　　Supply baith sauce and pickle.

But now the tumbler smokes,
　　Remove the wine decanter ;
Then runs the stream of jokes,
　　Wi' light and pleasant banter,
And Humour bright unfolds
　　Her rich and racy story ;
Or in Music's voice is told
　　Old Scotland's martial glory.

Deep in fishing lore
　　Some discourse on tackle,
Intently poring o'er
　　Stores o' gut and hackle.
Plans to guard the Tweed
　　Some are busy broaching,
And save the saumon breed
　　Frae the pest of poaching.

And should debate grow keen,
　　Some all-absorbing chorus
Will, rising o'er the din,
　　To harmony restore us ;
Or Edmunds' manly voice,
　　Filling all the valley,
Make every heart rejoice
　　With " Sally in our Alley."

But now the hour of ten
　　Tells 'tis time to settle ;
And we must now refrain
　　To order in the kettle.
The cauld invites to sleep—
　　Then, Robert, gie's a ca', man,
At the mornin's peep,
　　In time to catch a saumon.

The Killing of a Salmon.

TUNE—"*Calder Fair.*"

ANGLERS all give ear to me
　Till I relate a story,
That happened on the bonnie Tweed
　When rolling in its glory.

It was in eighteen-forty-nine,
　When fishing wi' the rod and line,
On the Elm-Weil, ae' night sae fine,
　I hooked a muckle Salmon.

Up and down the Pool he rush'd
　Wi' railway speed, I'm sure, man,
But aye's I tried to pull him out,
　He said nane o' your gammon.

I hae nae doubt you'd pull me out,
　Were I not up to snuff, man ;
But a' your skill against my will,
　Ye'll find its not enough, man.

We had a tussle ance before,
　As I went to the sea, man ;
I broke you then—I'll do't again—
　In the twinkling of an e'e, man.

You think you have me in a fix,
    But you're not up to a' my tricks ;
Your braw new rod I'll break to sticks,
    Or e'er ye conquer me, man.

Ye needna craw sac crouse, says I,
    Nor shake your head nor wink your eye,
Your boasted strength I mean to try,
    Or e'er I let you free, man.

The scaly buffer rushed about,
    I rolled him in, I let him out,
Amang the stanes he bored his snout,
    Determined to be free, man.

His silvery sides began to show
    All glittering in the sun, man,
That showed to me his watery course
    Would very soon be run, man.

Wi' clip in hand, I took my stand,
    I held him tight, and thought all right,
But, by my troth, he took a fright,
    And off he went again, man.

That's right says I, with mirth and glee,—
    'Tis your last effort to get free,—
His strength was gone, as I could see,
    So I hauled him in and clipt him.

The Doctor and the Professor.

THE following lines are extracted from the Club's Album, as a specimen of the free and good humoured tone pervading the relations between the members. The late Dr Skae, long medical officer in the Morningside Asylum, was the writer. He discourses of himself and of his brother member, the late Professor Henderson. The allusion to an *apology* had reference to the circumstance that Professor Henderson practised homœopathy, and this had caused considerable professional separation from many of his brethren, all of whom, however, had the highest respect for him personally, and for his eminent talents, especially as a pathologist.

The Doctor and the Professor.

On the twenty-eighth of Februairy,
A man, both fat, and very hairy
About the face, came to the Nest,
To fish with Morton and the rest.

He was a Doctor Psychological,
More rational than theological,
Mad Doctor still they say he is,
As any one sees from his phiz.

He fished with the renowned professor,
(Not the *fly*, but the *Chair's* possessor)
Of the class called Pathology,
Attending which needs an apology.

The Professor's rod, although a tried one,
Was not so lucky as the buyed one
Which the Doctor got from Robert,
A bran new London one by Hobert.

The doctors twain then joined the *Scotsman*,
And Morton, that confounded sportsman,
In dining, drinking, singing, spouting,
And applauding their great feats with shouting.

Ye Lamente of Ye Fraser.

One of the most talented and brilliant men who have been members of the Club—the late lamented Kenmure Maitland —was the author of the following soliloquy. It was com- posed after one of the contests for the Club's medal. The medal goes annually, after a competition open to all members of the Club, to him who has caught the largest weight of Salmon, and he retains it for a year. The soliloquy is put into the mouth of a respected member, who is equally famous for his perseverance, and his skill and success, in angling. He has gained the medal much oftener than any other mem- ber of the Club. Besides this principal hero of the poem, many of the other members (in 1864) are very happily in- troduced.

Ye Lamente of Ye Fraser.

ONCE more I have lost! Foul fall this fatal day,
 That any other should have borne away
The prize, which I, alas ! too fondly, guessed
Again would glitter on my manly breast !
But no ! the gods—I mean the fates and fishes—
Have not responded to my fervent wishes ;
And now on me it has devolved to tell
The haps and mishaps that each one befell.

But, how it riles me ! for I made so sure,
That I this prize would easily secure.
Did I not come here three whole days ago,
And fish each yard of water, high and low,
To find what fly the fish just now affect,
And where the best success I might expect ?
Capricious brutes !   They lured me on at first,
To make my failure now the more accurst.
I had on Thursday such a glorious haul,—
Five noble fish, weight, seventy pounds in all.
Hang and confound it ! what a grievous fool,
Not to have tethered, in some secret pool,
Some of those monsters I was wrong to slay,
And should have kept convenient for to-day !
To think how easily I might have tied
Two of the biggest, anchored side by side,
Then in the Putt of " Arris,"[1] there each lies,
To win my *bets, eh !* and to prig the prize !
While here, to-day, I've not one single fin !
But my recital let me now begin.

I was alone here on the Thursday night,
Flushed with success, and expectations bright ;
My heart beat high, and so, to cheer my body,
I took that night one extra glass of toddy.
Maitland[2] came out by next day's forenoon train,
And tried his luck—of course 'twas all in vain.

---

[1] " Arris Putt " is a deep running stream in the Fernielee waters, famed
for " holding " large fish.
[2] Mr Maitland, the author of this piece, was Sheriff-Clerk of Mid-Lothian,
and was tall and thin.

That high official—that official tall—
Soon found his skill, compared with mine, was small.
Official knowledge he finds "all my cye,"
Of-fish-all knowledge, when he comes to try.
His basket had *Moll Thomson's*[1] mark at eve,
While I'd a fresh-run fish his soul to grieve.
Simson[2] and Edmunds,[3] they cam' late yestreen, —
Red were their noses, for the frost was keen ;
Stewart came with them—his nose too was red,
And grew no paler ere the hour for bed.
Edmunds had on a bandit-looking hat
(We argued something desperate from that) ;
And, well wound round with casting lines and
    flies,
It really looked like bidding for the prize.
His air so jaunty seemed to me to say, Sir,
Come on, Macduff, I'm ready for *thee, Fraser!*
Our dear friend David wore his usual smile,
(That true Nathaniel, for in him no guile),
And yet I bore him an unchristian grudge,
For which I had some reason, ye will judge.
You know the prize last year from me he took,
Winning it basely by a shabby fluke—
By half a pound his fish in weight beat mine ;
But, what a fish his was !   Why, Pharaoh's kine

---

[1] " Moll Thomson's mark "—M. T. (*empty*).
    The late Mr David Simson, of the Royal Scottish Academy, a genial and much loved member of the Club.
[3] Mr Edmunds is a teacher of music and a keen fisher, whose sweet songs have often cheered the social meetings of the Club.

Were nought in leanness to that wretched kelt,
And, oh ! ye gods, how awfully it smelt !![1]

Morton[2] and Henderson[3] came out next morn,
But not even then thought I my chance forlorn;
Although our worthy Preses fishes well,
And casts, o'er men and fish, with potent spell,
Alluring links, attractively, that win
Both heart and fancy, and both hand and fin.
But where M'Gibbon,[4] Forrest,[5] Caunter,[6] Skae ?[7]
The first takes *Council* to remain away.
Let him remain at home, then, if he please,
And golden chances lose for *guilded* ease.
Then Forrest, our illustrious illustrator,
Has *graver* reasons that detain him later ;
Besides, he grumbles that his " back does ache ;"
Caunter said " No," for *contra*diction's sake ;
Skae has *ske*daddled with his big brown beard,
'Tis just as lucky, else the fish were *scared.*

[1] In the previous year's competition, Mr Simson caught the only fish—a very poor one—and gained the medal.

[2] Mr Charles Morton, W.S., who was then, and still is, President of the Club.

[3] Professor Henderson.

[4] Mr Charles M'Gibbon, who was then Dean of Guild, and a member of the Town Council.

[5] Mr William Forrest, engraver, one of the princes of his art, who has executed the illustrations for this volume. He is one of the few remaining original members of the Club.

[6] The late Mr Robert Caunter, of the Royal Scottish Academy, a man of rare humour, and the designer of many of the sketches engraved for this volume by Mr Forrest. The illustration at the head of this piece is from his pencil. His imitations of opera singing will not soon be forgotten by those who enjoyed them at the " Nest."

[7] Dr Skae.

And why are absent both the Brothers Menzies ?[1]
Well ! I suppose the reason of the thing is,
Tom's no keen fisher, so he stays awa';
And George, whose title is " The Grand Bashaw,"
Could not expect to gain, yet feared to lose,
So did not come, because—he did not choose!
George, somehow, seldom *does* a fish secure,
Unless with Robert at his elbow, sure ;—
In fact, he thinks he fishes quite enough,
If he looks on—and takes a pinch of snuff.

But all of these might come and fish their fill,
As well as Arkley,[2] Royal Steuart,[3] Hill,
And others, who judiciously abstain
From enterprises with no hope of gain.
There's only one of all our Members' roll
Who has the power to damp my ardent soul.
Anxious, I listen for the usual bustle
That hails the advent of th' Immortal Russel ;[4]
For who so famous by the Tweed's fair banks
As he who plays there such prodigious pranks ?
Has not each stretch, from Berwick to the source,
Full oft resounded to his shouting hoarse,

[1] Mr Thomas Menzies, shipowner, Edinburgh, and Mr George Menzies, shipbuilder, Leith.
[2] Mr Arkley was then Sheriff of Mid-Lothian.
[3] Mr Steuart, of the Exchequer, dubbed "Royal" from a fancied resemblance to Prince Charles, and to distinguish him from the author of the " Art of Angling," an enthusiastic member of the Club.
[4] The much loved and deeply lamented Editor of the *Scotsman*, a keen and successful angler, and the soul of many never-to-be-forgotten social meetings at the "Nest."

As, rushing, dashing, plashing through its tide,
He bawls for help to all the country side?
Kipper, and Kelt, and *Cod*, have spread his fame,
(See *Border Beacon* for report of same).[1]
Uproarious Russel! full of life and noise,
Most buoyant spirit, where we all are boys—
Glorious while fishing, glorious eating, drinking,
And glorious while inditing and while thinking;
But silent never—even in his bed!
Aye, he's the man I'm most inclined to dread,
For he's so jealous of my greater skill,
That, if I beat him, he would take it ill;
And, in his rage against a nobler sportsman,
He might put something frantic in the *Scotsman*.
However, he from coming was prevented—
As well for him!—and I was well contented.

Lowe,[2] by the way, who stays at Caddonlee,
Sent down his henchman all the way, to see
What possible arrangement might be made
To give him water where he need not wade.
I hear he was so modest as suggest
"Neidpath" and "Gullets" would befit him best,
But, though most delicately put by Linton,
We were not quite inclined to act this hint on.

---

[1] An extract from the *Border Beacon* which follows, gives a lively account of the ludicrous incident referred to, which actually occurred, and at the time moved the Editor to much wrath.

[2] The late Mr Lowe, teacher of dancing, an accomplished angler, who was always ready to give his advice, and (not so common) his flies, to a younger member. He was at the time in lodgings at Caddonlee, on the banks of the Tweed, and had a river side fisher, and accomplished poacher, who is now handed down to future fame, as his henchman.

The hour of starting now approaches fast,
Pools are divided, and the lots are cast;
I hoped for Neidpath—but I won it not—
To Henderson and Stewart went that lot;
The upper stretch is Edmunds' and Lowe's,
Simson and I have Elm-Weil and the Trows,
Morton and Maitland they get all the rest,
And off we set, each one with eager zest.
(I saw that Stewart thought he'd do me quite,
But I'd as many fish as he, at night.)
While all were getting ready rods and flies,
My cast was scanned with scrutinising eyes;
But did they think I was so precious green,
As let my real fav'rite hook be seen?
And yet, precautions, dodges, skill are vain,
When fickle fortune wills you not to gain.
The day was bright, the water low and clear,
And calm and frosty was the atmosphere;
Lovely the tints on Yair and Fernielee,
But all their loveliness was *tint* on me!
I saw but one fish all that weary day,—
A twenty-pounder,—in the Elm-Weil[1] play,
I raised him, hooked him, held him, thought I'd
        nicked him,
But he broke off, and *I* was left the victim.
Molly! why *did* you then let go my hair,
And leave me such an image of despair?

The shades of night were closing darkly o'er,
As one by one we reach the cottage door.

[1] A famed salmon pool above Yair Bridge.

Henderson first arrives, in triumph great,
Bringing two fish, and keen to know his fate.
He sees one sorry fish, with Simson's name,
Laid on the box, which his two put to shame ;
Of course 'twas David's, for who else would own
A vile red-herring-looking thing like yon,
Twin-brother sodger to his last year's one ?
David comes next and swears there was a job,
A scurvy plot, 'twixt Henderson and Rob,
Who saw a big fish in the Boat-pool play,
And watched there till the former came that way.
When David passed, says Rob, in pawky style,
" Wall ! Maister Samson, 'tisna worth your while
To fish the Boat-pool, gae an' try the Bogle."
There he gets yon (enough to make a rogue ill),
While the Professor, coming by and bye,
Catches the one old Robert kept so sly—
A fifteen-pounder ; then his other prize,
From Neidpath taken, weighs full half that size.
At each death-struggle Stewart was at hand,
And lent his aid to bring the fish to land.
But at the Boat-pool something rare occurred,
Which, with the serious, mingled the absurd.
The man who fishes salmon with a Bob,
True anglers look on rather as a snob.
Well ! not to put on it a point too fine,
Henderson this day had one on his line ;
And in the Boat-pool as his fish he played,
And Stewart keenly rushes to his aid,
The bob-hook caught the latter by the nose,
(Feelingly now he knows a fish's woes)

P

Which gave our author, as that fish was dangling,
Practical *new* hints in the art of angling !
Then, by the margin of that Pool, I ween,
Were *three* well-hooked proboscces to be seen—
Yes ! Stewart's with the Salmon's, on the cast,
And the *Professor's*—not the least though last !
Did not that beak foreshadow long ago,
By hook and crook that he'd defeat each foe ?[1]

Stewart, poor soul ! had nothing of his own,
A fish hooked him, but he, alas ! hooked none.
Morton's return, and Maitland's also, *nil,*—
So they take drams all round, they feel so ill.
But here comes Edmunds, tramping from afar,
And puffing proudly at a huge cigar ;
With air heroic he puts down his rod,
And swings his bag from off his shoulders broad ;
The bag is opened, the contents we view,
A well-made gaucy fish of silver hue,
None of your sodgers, fiery red as mullets,
A clean-run eighteen-pounder from the Gullets.
But as the Medal goes to greatest weight,
Edmunds submits, though sadly, to his fate.
We hear from him, Lowe had not e'en a rise,
And, more than that, he lent to Edmunds flies
With which the latter, 'neath his very nose,
Killed this fine fish, and hooked one more that rose.

[1] The incident actually occurred. Mr Stewart was the author of "The Art of Angling." He was himself a first-rate angler, and was then Secretary of the Club. The Professor's nose was Slawkenbergian and considerably *hooked.*

But Lowe can spare a feather from the crest
That crowns his brow, as Nestor of "The Nest."

As for our Nosological Professor—
Whose chance we thought of all so much the lesser—
A good hand he, perhaps, at Diagnosis,
But not the Salmon-fisher he supposes ;
Talents we grant him, highly professorial,
But deem him student in the Piscatorial.
Yet so it happens, from capricious whim,
The fickle goddess has selected him
This year to wear the honours of our Club ;
Still it consoles me, as I feel the rub,
That neither Russel, Morton, nor *the Sec,*
Wear that blue ribbon dangling from their neck.
But come, that merely is a private groan,
Henderson won it fairly, we must own ;
And he has promised, for our next year's feast,
Of Mumm's champagne a dozen at the least ;
And if he *doesn't* (although doubt's absurd)
He may be sure that *mum* is not the word
With which we shall our sentiments express—
Professors must fulfil what they profess.
But here's his health, great happiness and fees ;
Now, gentlemen, a bumper, if you please !

Not a Clever Capture.

[The following is the article in the *Border Beacon*, referred
to in "Ye Lamente."]

THE gripe of the law being so far relaxed as to allow rod
fishing for salmon to begin on Monday, not a few of the lovers
of the angle, and of those several city-winter-pent wielders of
the rod, were all agog by "Tweed's" (anything but) silvery
stream by skreigh o' day.   Among those, generalised elsewhere,
as doomed to disappointment by a risen and rising water, was
one member of the Fourth Estate, who wields, with equal
potency and dire effect, the rod and the quill.   Returning home
in no very placable mood, he arrived at one of the smaller
railway stations in the afternoon, and depositing his (not
empty) bag in the station, he took a saunter to view, with one
more look of disgust, the red roaring flood.   Meanwhile two
men in blue and silver, with glazed caps and overalls—the
well-known livery of the Tweed police—arrive at the station,
and the elder and more sagacious of the two is attracted
towards the bag, either by its appearance, or " its ancient fish-
like smell."   Rendered thus bold, he ventures to approach
and handle with sacrilegious fingers the private property of
the Man of Letters.   Winking to his friend, he chucklingly
whispered, "It's a' richt"—("wrong" he meant)— "there's
a fish in the bag!"   Nothing more was said.   The train draws
up; the limbs of the law and their unsuspecting victim walk
into the same compartment, the latter carrying with him his
trusty bag—the companion of many a bloody foray by the
Tweed.   No sooner had the train started than a hint was
dropped by the bailiffs, that "they had sufficient ground to

suspect " something illegal was in the bag, and a request was made to have it opened, which the Redacteur, like a man of honour, of innocence, and a gentleman, resisted, as a most un-warranted interference with his private property. Expostula-tions and threats were equally in vain. The canvass was unstrapped—whether violently or not—when behold !—*Monstrum, horrendum, informe, ingens cui lumen ademptum!* Neither a goodly new-run grey kipper, nor a foul flabby kelt, met the bewildered eyes alike of the myrmidons and the passengers, but a great *cod's head and shoulders*, gaping out on all with a gashly grin, and, to the eye of fancy, with a faint twinkle of a wink in its dim lack-lustre eyes ! Of course, while the gravity of the spectators was fairly upset by this ludicrous episode, the faces of the bailiffs became wonderfully elongated, and they skedaddled at the first station; while the wrath of the owner was, like that of Achilles, something unappeasable, and dreadful to behold. The cod had been purchased by himself, in the hope of spending a few pleasant days of sport in his snug country retreat, where the brawling Tweed below incessantly, in the fishing season, lulls the wearied anglers to repose, after their hard fought day's work. But alas for the hopes of the salmon fisher in this blowy, rainy, snowy, cold, and floody month ! The river being unfishable, our friend deemed it prudent to retire to town, and, like an economic husband and father of a family, he was carrying back with him his uneaten dinner, when the above comical adventure took place, at which, we know well, no one will laugh more heartily than himself, when his wrath is mellowed down by time, and he relates it to his friends in the " snuggery " after a well fished day.

Roar from a Kelt.

THE Editor, of whose adventures so much is told in what immediately precedes, did not despise, when clean fish were not in the waters of the Nest, the capture of a lean and hungry kelt. He *must* fish for something, and it was all he could get at that time of the year. Naturally the kelts object, and they make their moan in the following "Roar from a Kelt."

Roar from a Kelt.

THE kelt catcher's coming, oh dear ! oh dear !
The kelt catcher's coming, oh dear !
He'll slaughter us wholly, that's clear, quite clear,
I've a warning, which puts me in fear, in fear.

The lord of the streams he will kill, will kill,
His basket with baggits he'll fill, he'll fill,
And the blood of foul fish he'll spill, he'll spill,
With minnows he takes from the rill, the rill.

The clean fish he knocks on the brains, the brains,
    His hooks with kelt's blood he stains, he stains,
Disregarding the poor brute's pains, its pains,
    As he to the Bailiff explains, explains.

The sea trout he jumps at his fly, rash, rash !
    He flounders, then rolls ou his side, splash, splash,
At last goes the gaff through his sides, crash, crash.
    What a mercy it settles his hash, his hash.

Not a salmon or sea-trout in Tweed, in Tweed,
    Is safe from the kelt catcher's greed, his greed ;
He pulls them in slyly with speed, with speed,
    Afraid to be caught in the deed, the deed.

Perhaps we were made with intent, intent,
    That hooks through our jaws should be sent, be
       sent,
Our nerves were contrived to be rent, be rent,
    And our lives to be tortured were meant, were
       meant.

If this is the case as I fear, I fear,
    Of course 'tis all right, though 'tis rather queer ;
And to put us to use in our sphere, our sphere,
    A. Russel is coming, oh dear ! oh dear !

Reminiscences of a Veteran Angler.

I'VE been a fisher a' my days,
And dearly like the fisher's ways ;
Whether on stream, in cot, or ha',
With genial hearts you'll find them a'.
I've fished the Esks, baith South and North.
The Eden, Leven, Teith, and Forth,
The three that out frae Hartfell glide—
The Tweed, the Annan, and the Clyde—
The Ettrick, Yarrow, and the Lyne,
The Gala, Heriot, and the Tyne ;
The Lochs of Mary, Lowes, and Skene,
And mony a burn and stream between ;
But for good sport, and cheer and jest,
Commend me to the Robin's Nest.

The Trial.

IT is difficult to believe that anything but envy, or, as it may be termed, " that stern *hate* which anglers feel " towards a too successful brother, would have induced such a *Lybell* as the following upon the accomplished fisher who was celebrated in "Y⁰ Lamente." At another competition he won the medal, having got the only fish that was captured. But as no skill, however great, and no patience, however prolonged, can ensure that the fish the angler induces to rise shall be a good one, it happened, on the occasion in question, that the capture was certainly not an inviting specimen of the genus Salmo. Neither it nor its captor were, however, so very unworthy, as is represented in this supposed trial.

Apud Rubeculæ Nidulum,
Die Veneris Novembri Secundo, 1867,
Curia legitime affirmata.

Intran ALEXANDER PHRASIOR, *Typographus, in Foro*
Piscatorio Veterano Angiportu.

INDICTED AND ACCUSED:

THAT WHEREAS by Act of Her Majesty Victoria, vicesimo et vicesimo uno, entituled "The Tweed Fisheries Act 1857," section 70, it is enacted, that "Every person who, during the periods in each year when it is lawful to fish for Salmon, knowingly takes or kills, or aids or assists in taking or killing, in or from the River any Foul, Unclean, or Unseasonable Salmon," shall be liable in the penalties therein set forth: YET TRUE IT WAS AND OF VERITY, that the said ALEXANDER PHRASIOR was guilty of the said Crime, actor or art in part, IN AS MUCH AS,

On Friday the Second Day of November 1867,

or on one or other of the days of that month, or of October immediately preceding, or of December immediately following, he the said ALEXANDER PHRASIOR did, wilfully, knowingly, and feloniously, take, from the said river, and kill, in or about the place or cast called the GULLETS,

A Foul, Unclean, and Unseasonable Salmon,

and having so taken and killed the same, did thereupon, falsely and vain-gloriously, and with most intolerable iteration, assert and declare that he, the said ALEXANDER PHRASIOR, had, as the taker and killer of said Foul, &c., brute, been the successful competitor for the Medal of the EDINBURGH ANGLING CLUB, which was that day competed for. And the same being admitted by the Panel, or duly proved, he ought to be amerced and punished in terms of Law, to deter all others from committing the like crimes in time coming.

The Panel pleaded Not Guilty; and the following Assize was empanelled and sworn—

> EDMUND EDMUNDS,
> THOMAS MENZIES,
> DAVID SIMSON,
> JOHN McKIE,
> JAMES STEEL,
> WILLIAM HANDYSIDE, and
> A Lot More.

ROBERT SHORTREDE, the Officer of Court, being called on to produce the *corpus delicti*, produced the same, whereupon the Gentlemen of Assize shut up their noses, and the windows of the Court were wide opened.

The said ROBERT SHORTREDE, being sworn and examined deponed—That he had known Salmon, and every other kind of fish, from infancy, and a good while before. That he was not certain if the *corpus delicti* was a Salmon or other fish, but if it was, it was the most foulest, uncleanest, and most unseasonablest Salmon that he had ever seen or heard of, in this world or any other. That the said brute was brought to him by the Panel, who repeatedly declared that he had caught and killed the same, and was thereby entitled to the Medal. That he had seen many bad fish killed by improper and unprincipled Members of the Club; and recollected one commonly called a "Sodger" killed by David Simson; but that Sodger was a perfect beauty compared with the brute now polluting the air of the Court House.

Examined by Panel.—" Will you swear, Sir, that that *is* a Fish ?"—" Waal, I'm no sae guid at swearin' as R—ss—l,[1] an' I'm no free to say that it's a fish noo, but I'll swear before

---

[1] Our worthy keeper is sometimes not very particular in his language when speaking of members. On one occasion, the Editor and the writer of this note had fished for a long day without seeing a fish. Towards evening both had set their minds on fishing the "Boat Pool," close to the "Nest" to which they were about to retire. The Editor reached it first, so the other passed on to cast his fly in "Neidpath," a pool a little above, where, by unwonted good luck, he hooked and killed a couple of beauties in a very few minutes. Returning to the Boat Pool, he found the Editor just leaving, not having seen a fish. Getting into the pool he commenced to fish, and when his friend had got far enough away (to his shame be it said, he was fishing with a *Bob*), he called to Robert to put the two dead fish on his hooks, which was done. A tremendous hulloo was then got up, which brought the Editor rushing back. A frantic encounter between the fisher and the fish was then enacted, in which it was at last disclosed that *two* fish were "on," to the dismay and rage of the Editor, who expressed his feelings in ejaculations of a somewhat strong description. Ultimately he was allowed to see that both fish were dead, when excited expressions of direst import followed, and his wrath reached a climax when Robert quietly remarked,—" Waal, I never seed Russel fairly dune afore ! "

On another occasion, Robert was asked by a member who had just arrived, what others were at the Nest. He replied in his own vernacular—" Ou, there's the twa Samsons, and the body Arkley, and *his clerk* "—thus unceremoniously designating two eminent members of the Royal Scottish Academy, the Sheriff of Mid-Lothian, and the *Sheriff*-Clerk.

onybody that the thing was ance a fish of the Salmon kind, though it's sair disguised by auld age and beasts about it's gills. I never before seed sic an awfu' brute at the "Ast."

The Court and Jury unanimously declared that they were clean done with anxiety, and the smell of the "thing." They. liquored up, in which the unfortunate Panel, with a levity which showed him to be insensible to the sinfulness of the estate into which he had fallen, largely joined.

JOHN KYD, Merchant, Leith, deponed—I fished the Gullets on the day libelled, from eleven till one o'clock. Panel came down about one, and began to fish. Saw him hook the thing produced, but did not know what it was. It conducted itself in a very extraordinary manner—never saw a clean fish behave as it did. Panel, after he got it out, killed it by repeated kicks with his feet, which had upon them large heavy boots. He never proposed to put it back into the river.

Cross-examined by Panel.—I assisted Panel to land the fish.

Re-examined.—I did so only because Panel asked me. I did not know its condition, till after it was landed, or I would have refused to touch it even with a pair of tongs. Landed it with a landing-net which was supplied by Panel. Have deeply regretted it ever since. Would much rather have put Panel into the river, than have taken fish out, if I had had time to gather my wits—which are very frequently not altogether at my command.

At this stage,

McKIE, the Juror, got up and said he was "like to swear," and having sworn copiously, deponed—That he is tenant of a fishing in the Dee, near Kirkcudbright, and has an intimate personal acquaintance with foul fish, from daily intercourse with them in that river. The "thing" produced he has no doubt is a fish, but it is one in the very last stage of uncleanness. In his extensive experience of that sort of thing, he never saw or heard of one so bad—certainly never in the Dee. He added that it might almost be taken for a newly spawned Cod, and concluded, in some excitement, "that it was d—d bad."

The Panel addressed the Court, pleading that, on the evidence adduced, the "thing" libelled was proved not to be a fish at all. He also stated that some witnesses as to character were in attendance; but that, after having communicated with them, privately, he was satisfied that he would act wisely in not bringing them forward.

The Jury unanimously found the Panel Guilty as libelled, and recommended him to the most unmerciful sentence the Court could pronounce.

The Panel here moved, in arrest of judgment, that the whole proceedings are void, as the day libelled is Friday, and as the Record bears that Friday was the day on which the Court was held, whereas the day is Saturday.

The Court held that the day was quite immaterial—the essence of the charge being whether the fish was killed; not on what day it was killed; and the Panel would soon find to his cost that the Court is sitting, whether this is Friday or Saturday.

The Presiding Judge, under much emotion, finished his tumbler, and pronounced sentence as follows :—Fines and amerciates the Panel in the sum of Five Pounds Sterling, and grants warrant for instant execution against the body and goods of the Panel ; confiscates the Rod, Reel, and Landing

Net of the Panel, and authorizes the Officer of Court to take possession of and sell the same, and convert the price into liquor.   Further ordains the "thing" to be burnt by his hands, as the Common Hangman *pro tempore.*

VIVAT REGINA.

Court adjourned.

Thereafter the Court and Jury unanimously found that the Competition for the Medal had failed, and fixed Saturday, the ninth of November, for a new Competition, to take place at eleven of the clock Forenoon.

THE PRESIDENT

HIS MARK.

Saumon.

AMONG the Poets who sing the praises of " Saumon " in our little volume, no one has delineated his beauty and his worth more happily than the author of the song which follows.   It is from the bright pen of an honorary member, equally famed for his medical and analytical skill, and the grace and delicacy of his lyrics, on any subject from the material " Marrow-Bone" to the sober cup of " Plain Cold Water " or the ethereal " Sweet Spirit of Chloroform."

Saumon.

AIR—"*Cauld Kail in Aberdeen.*"

THERE's haddies i' the Firth o' Forth,
   There's turbot big and sma', man ;
There's flukes—though they're but little worth—
   There's Caller ou' an' a, man.
But fish in shell, or fish in scale,
   Whate'er ye like't to ca', man,
There's nane can doot the very wale
   O' fishes is a Saumon.

There's herrin' catch'd aboot Dunbar,
   An' whitin's aff Skateraw, man ;
But wha sae daft as to compare
   The like o' them to Saumon.
The English folk like whitin's best,
   The Dutch eat herrin' raw, man ;
But ilka body to his taste,
   An' mine's content wi' Saumon.

Oh, mark him, rinnin' frae the tide,
   In blue and siller braw, man ;
The ticks upon his gaucy side
   Shaw him a new rin Saumon.

An' though he 'scape the Berwick net,
  The Duke at Floors, an' a', man,
There's mony a chance remainin' yet
  To catch that bonnie Saumon.

Across the Pool the fisher's flee
  Fa's licht as micht a straw, man ;
Soops doon the stream, an' syne a wee
  Hangs trem'lin' o'er the Saumon.
A moment mair—the line is stent—
  A rug, and then a draw, man ;
An' noo, the soople tap-piece bent,
  He's tackled wi' his Saumon.

Frae aff the birling reel the line
  Like lichtnin' spins awa', man ;
The fisher lauchs, for he kens fine
  He's heuked a guidly Saumon.
He's up, he's doon, he's here, he's there,
  Wi' mony a twist and thraw, man ;
Noo deep in Tweed, noo i' the air,—
  My troth, a lively Saumon.

But stren'th an' natur' for a while
  Can warstle against a', man ;
Yet natur' aft maun yield to guile,
  As weel in man as Saumon.
An' sae the merry fish, that rose
  To tak' that flee sae braw, man,
Noo sidelin's sooms at his life's close—
  A worn an' deein' Saumon.

Wi' ready gaff the callant stan's,
　　The fish ashore to draw, man ;
The fisher bids him haud his han's,
　　An' no to hash his Saumon.
" He's clean dune oot ; gae grup the tail,
　　Just whar it tapers sma', man,
An' lan' him up baith safe an' hale,"—
　　My word, a bonnie Saumon !

Gae bid the lass set on the pat,
　　An' see its no owre sma', man,
An' pit twa goupens in o' saut,
　　To boil my bonnie Saumon ;
An' sen' for Jock, an' Rab, an' Tam,—
　　They're fishers ane an' a', man,—
An' bid them come to me at hame,
　　An' eat my bonnie Saumon.

The gentry get their cooks frae France,
　　Wi' mony a queer kickshaw, man ;
But, haith, I wadna tak' their chance,
　　When I hae sic a Saumon !
Wi' it, an' some o' Scotland's best,
　　A cheerer—maybe twa, man—
We'll gang like decent folk to rest,
　　An' dream o' catchin' Saumon.

I ance was dinin' i' the toun,
　　Whar a'thing is sae braw, man,
An' there I saw a Lunnon loon
　　Eat Labster sauce wi' Saumon !

Wae's me ! that sic a slaister suid
    Gang into mortal maw, man,
To fyle the stamac'—spile the fuid—
    An' siccan fuid as Saumon !

Wi' flesh as pink as rose in June,
    Wi' curd as white as snaw, man,
An' sappy broe they boilt him in—
    Oh ! that's what I ca' Saumon !
To my best frein' I canna wish
    That better suid befa', man,
Than just to hae as guid a dish,
    As we hae wi' our Saumon.

To Scotland's ilka honest son,
    Her dochters fair an' a', man ;
To a' wha lo'e the rod and gun,
    We'll drink wi' a hurra', man !
May they frae mony sportin' days
    Baith health an' pleesur' draw, man ;
May Muircocks craw on a' the braes,
    The rivers swarm wi' Saumon !

The Salmon Clean.

AIR—" *The Ivy Green.*"

OH ! a gallant fish is the Salmon clean,
 As he springs in his silvery pride,
O'er the foaming cauld, when the Tweed runs deep,
 With a spate, in the wild March-tide.
Like a stout steel bow his back he bends ;
 Then, bright as the crescent-moon,
Leaps high in the air, this racer fair,
 And flasheth away full soon !
   Spinning along, when the spate rolls keen—
   A racer bold is the Salmon clean !

An angry fish is the Salmon clean,
 When he feeleth the sting of the fly,
Whose rainbow wings, as they danced so light,
 Attracted his roving eye.
Down ! with the speed of a startled steed,
 And up ! like a car of steam,—
He cleaves through the current, and dauntlessly stems
 The rush of the strongest stream.
   Darting quick, where the braes grow green—
   A wrathful fish is the Salmon clean !

A sulky fish is the Salmon clean,
  When he sinks like a lump of lead;
And lies in the depths of a swirling pool,
  Till you'd almost deem him dead.
You may pebbles fling, till your temper's gone,
  But never a fin stirs he;
Till you give him the spur—then with flash and birr
  He's away for the deep green sea.
      Sulking where no light is seen—
      A stiff old brute is the Salmon clean!

A bonnie fish is the Salmon clean,
  New beached on the pebbly shore,
With gasping gills, and a shuddering tail,
  That will furrow the flood no more.
The purple glaze on his shoulder thick,
  And the gleam of his silvery side,
As the vanquished hero swooning dies,
  Thrill the fisher's heart with pride;
      Gleaming bright in his silvery sheen—
      A Prince among Fins is the Salmon clean!

A dainty fish is the Salmon clean,
  As he swims in the seething brine,
Till his silver mail grows as soft as silk,
  And he melts into tears divine.
With rose-leaf flakes and curd of snow
  He tenderly woos us to dine;

But to him *one* kiss of the brimming *quaich*
  Is worth *ten* of the cold red wine.
    Steaming sweet on an ashet, I ween,
    The King of Fish is the Salmon clean.

An ill-faured fish is the Kelt unclean,
  As he hungrily hurries down,
To taste the spray of the salt-sea wave,
  And sport mid the oar-weed brown.
He'll take your fly, as it dances nigh,
  For he'd grab at a mouse or a flea ;
But out with the hook ! and tumble him in !
  He'll be back from the deep green sea !
    Ebony-black, and like serpent lean,
    A gruesome fish is the Kelt unclean !
    Oh Kelpie, that rulest o'er Tweed as Queen,
    Defend all rods from the Kelt unclean !

The Brig o' Yair.

AIR –" *When the Kye comes Hame.*"

Come all ye jolly anglers,
　Wha bide at Robin's Nest—
Your coat of arms[1] the wadin' trews,
　A Saumon flee your crest—
What scents the simmer gloamin',
　When the west is fadin' fair,
Like a whiff o' sweet tobacco,
　On the bonnie brig o' Yair!

As the crimson melts to rose,
　And the rose dissolves to grey,
And the mavis, in the snowy thorn,
　Lilts a hymn to deein' day;
Nae flouir can waft an odour
　Like this breath beyond compare—
Oh! the sweet whiff o' tobacco,
　On the bonnie brig o' Yair!

When the creel lies burstin' open
　Wi' its walth o' gowden spoil,
And the slender rod is restin'
　Frae its day o' deadly toil,

[1] Or legs.

What soothes the wearied fisher,
   As he coonts his dizzens there,
Like a whiff o' sweet tobacco,
   On the bonnie brig o' Yair !

Fair Tweed rins wimplin' through
   Wi' her voice o' siller chime,
An' she sings o' Scott and Scotland
   In the merry Border time ;
But her sang wad lose its subtlest charm,
   Withoot the fragrance rare
O' that whiff o' sweet tobacco,
   On the bonnie brig o' Yair !

They may prate o' Indian spices,
   And violets o' the sooth—
Let lovers rave o' hinnied bliss
   Culled frae a lassie's mooth—
Gie me the kiss o' pipe or weed
   When day is deein' fair,
And I'll woo the simmer gloamin',
   On the bonnie brig o' Yair !

Auld time maun frost the fisher's pow,
   Like that o' common men,
And rust the limbs, sae souple ance,
   Till they hirple but an' ben ;
Wi' lyart locks and feckless foot
   I'd totter frae my chair,
To blaw the sweet tobacco,
   On the bonnie brig o' Yair.

Autographs in the Club Album.

Visited The West, July 30, 1869

Jefferson Davis — Mississippi

C. Mackay — Fern Dell — Derby.

Hettie Nussel, Attuchbuch

i. Alex Russel Do

The Old Nest and the New.

BRIEF mention is made in the preface to this volume of the change of abode of the Edinburgh Angling Club. For fully 20 years the Club were tenants of the Ferniclee fishings, and of a quaint but snug and picturesque little cottage opposite Yair House,—the cottage so often alluded to in the songs as the "Robin's Nest," or, in Robert's tongue, "*The Axt.*" Many happy and deeply cherished associations will ever linger in the minds of those who enjoyed the social meetings at the Nest ; recalling the racy and rollicking fun and humour, and the stories and varied talk of Russel; the bright wit and happy puns of Maitland ; the mellowed liveliness and sweet warblings of dear and genial David Wylie, and the more resounding songs of Edmunds ; the drolleries, and the grotesque sayings and doings, and operas of Caunter ; and the happy hilarity and good humour of all. By every one who had the privilege of sharing in these symposia, they will be remembered as the *Noctes Cænæque Deum.*

Sad is it to think that so many of these bright spirits are with us no more.

Nor were these symposia confined to ourselves. Friends of like minds, and like pursuits, often joined us at our nest, who look back with warm feelings on many joyous evenings ; and though this volume is intended only for the work of members' pens, the reminiscences of one, who knew both the old Nest and the new one. and put his thoughts into its album after the old Nest had been forsaken, may not inappropriately be recorded here.

"THE CUCKOO IN THE NEST.

"TWEEDSIDE, *October* 19, 1875.

"'*She'll fesh! Eh, mon! She'll fesh the day!*' Oh, words of joy to the angler's ear as we come in sight of the beautiful and beloved Tweed! The speaker is Robert, the custodian of the 'Robin's Nest,' a man of few words, but of mighty piscatorial prowess, the guide and philosophic friend of those thrice-happy anglers who fish the Tweed. The feminine phrase which he uses in connection with the Tweed is partly a Scotch locution, and partly a term of affection. The river is called 'she' by those who know her best, and those who know her best love her most. The 'Robin's Nest' is a house on the river's bank, owned by a very exclusive and necessarily limited Club of Anglers, to whom it has for years been a place of rest, a refuge in time of trouble, a place of repose for weary heads, a little haven where human barks, more or less heavily laden with overwrought brains, cast anchor for a little while and are still. Scotchmen of note, as men of Law and of Letters, of Science and of Medicine, mighty wielders of the Pen and of the Pencil, have reason to love the 'Robin's Nest.' How many tender memories cling round it! How many pleasant recollections of happy days and happy evenings! What stories have been told, what songs have been sung, in its bright little dining-room, where the lamp swinging from the ceiling suggests all the snugness of a yacht's cabin, without any of its distressing associations! The walls are covered with sketches in water-colour, labours of love, made and presented by artists, members of the Club. Outside the windows are flower-beds blazing with colour, for the soil is good, the climate soft, and Robert is a famous gardener, directly descended from Adam—

who was a Scotchman. The air which comes in at the open
windows is heavy with the scent of roses, heliotrope, and mig-
nonette. Below the garden flows the silver Tweed, between its
high and thickly wooded banks, now in all their autumnal
glory. Pack up your burnt umber, and put away your sepia,
oh my brother of the brush! Your labour is in vain. Good
artist as you are, those tints are too gorgeous for even your
colour-box. A hundred shades of green, a hundred more of
brown, and as many of gold—how, vain man, will you
attempt to copy these, the glory of Tweedside, when we see

> ' Autumn laying here and there
> His fiery finger on the leaves.'

Right fronting the dining-room windows, but on the opposite
side of the river, is the house of Ashiestiel, whilome inhabited
by a magician, who made fairyland of all this country round
about, and whose name was WALTER SCOTT. Swelling up
behind, are the hills over which he strode, revolving his great
romances, *in imo pectore*, and working out the plans by which
he was to make himself laird of Abbotsford. That classic
pile is some four miles down the river, which just now
presents a succession of the loveliest views. The trees are in
all their panoply of colours. The heathery hills are of the
richest russet brown, brightened with wide patches of bronzed
fern. Every here and there birch-trees stand out like brazen
candelabra lighting up the hills. Autumn is here in all his
golden glory.

   "The object with which the Edinburgh Angling Club was
formed was 'to advance the delightful Science of Angling.'
The present 'Robin's Nest' is not the first Club-house. The
original 'Nest,' as the Members fondly call it, was a cottage
a short way further down the Tweed. There some of the

brightest days of the Club were spent; there keen wits flashed, and pleasant stories were told, and kindly banter and genial chaff made merry evenings, when the wet clothes were shuffled off, and the Anglers met to dine and talk over the day's sport. There good songs were sung, mostly written for the occasion, good stories were told, good toddies were drunk, and good tobaccos were smoked. Ah, those were piping days! —they were the golden prime! But the salt has not lost its savour. The original 'Nest' was, somewhat cruelly, one might think, taken away when the lease expired, and the merry Anglers were compelled to shift their quarters. The Robin flew a little further up-stream, and found a rest for the sole of his foot opposite Ashiesteel. Here, as befits the luxurious progress of the age, the Anglers made themselves a more pretentious and more roomy habitation, and to their new 'Nest' they removed their sketches and their books, and all the insignia and appurtenances of their idealized pastime. To this little spot come jaded writers and overworked lawyers, to let their poor brains lie fallow for a while. Come, too, artists, to gladden their eyes with fresh scenes of beauty, and to steep their souls in greenery. What good this 'Robin's Nest' has done to many of the most valuable intellects of the time, let their grateful memories attest. Two hours after he doffs his hot wig and gown in the Parliament House, the fagged-out pleader may be here at rest. The fevered man of letters or of science, who finds those dull pains behind his eyes and at the back of his head which give warning that the pressure has been too high and too long kept up, can leave his desk, and in a couple of hours be up to his middle in the Tweed, with the fresh air blowing on him down the valley, and blowing new life into him. Many a man who has made his mark, and worthily done his work in the world, owes something to the 'Robin's Nest.' Little wonder that the members prize it, and cling fondly to it and its associations! Little wonder that they make choice drawings to decorate its rooms, and write sweet and merry songs to be sung at its cheerful and temperate symposia!

"Here comes Robert with the rods and the 'waders,' the latter deplorably unbecoming garments, but indispensable. The human form is not made more divine by being clad in fishing costume. 'Batavian grace' is the prominent characteristic of an angler just before he steps into the Tweed. But see him as he wields his mighty rod, the graceful sweep of the right arm, by which he projects a vast length of line, and lets the fly just drop on the water, light and treacherous as the first dainty kiss on a maiden's cheek. Like a rock he stands firm in the rushing stream. With anxious eye he scans the water, drawing his line over every spot where he thinks a Salmon may be lurking. Patiently and perseveringly does he fish every yard of the river, until he arrives at one of the choicest casts. Then, the multitudinous virtues, which an angler must possess, have their reward. A sudden snatch sends a thrill of angelic joy up the line, down the rod, and into the fisherman's heart of hearts. 'I have him!' Then comes the tug of war! Up the stream, down the stream, across the stream, rushes the big fish! The reel creaks, the line spins out. Fast and furious is the struggle; but, sometimes giving, sometimes taking, always steadily keeping him on, the angler begins at last to wind him up. A silver streak is seen through the rushing stream, and, with a wild dash for freedom, the Salmon springs into the air, and falls back into the river with a splash. All in vain! and in five minutes more the shining creature is drawn gently to the bank, where Robert is waiting for him with the landing net. In half a minute twenty pounds weight of fish is gasping on the sward, and the angler knows one of those moments of supreme joy which are too seldom experienced by frail mortality. The sober test of the scales reduces the first sanguine estimate to seventeen pounds dead weight, but that in no way lessens the captor's pride and delight. By and by, he will accept with modesty the cordial congratulations of his brother Members, and all the evening will preserve the dignified demeanour of a conquering hero, conscious but not boastful.

"These are the calm delights of fair Tweedside, and these the cherished joys of the 'Robin's Nest.' Men may come and men may go, but Tweed flows on for ever; and so long as she flows may she always have a fish in the well-known casts, a jovial company of brother Anglers in her 'Robin's Nest,' and a perennial poet laureate to sing her charms in strains like these :—

> " ' Of all the bends on silver Tweed
>   Where is there one so fair,
> As that in front of Fernielee,
>   The famed Boat-pool of Yair ?
> The fringing trees droop tenderly
>   From banks of sward all green,
> And in the waters, passing by,
>   Their mirror'd grace is seen ;
> And when the summer zephyrs blow,
> And swing the branches hanging low,
>   Soft kisses pass between.' "

T

Unfortunately for the Club, other arrangements made it necessary for the landlord to take the fishings and the cottage into his own hands, and the Club had to leave their snuggery and to look for a "fresh home and fishings new." They got, through the kindness of the Laird of Torwoodlee, a stretch of water, including some of the sweetest reaches of the Tweed, and not a few good "pools" and "streams," with a lease of land sufficient to build a cottage, and to lay out a garden, and other pleasant surroundings, in which, if not possessing all the picturesque features of their Sedilia Antiqua, they have found more comfortable quarters. From it they can daily feast their eyes and their imaginations on the early home of the great Wizard of the North, Ashiestiel being on the banks of the Tweed immediately opposite. Still it was with a sore wrench that the Club extinguished the fires on the old hearths, loved by them as the Kaim of Derncleugh by old Meg. The memories of the "Nest," and the anticipated pleasures of the new residence, form the subject of the following verses; and in giving them a place, even in this private volume, it is only right to say that the somewhat vituperative allusions to the former landlord, under whom so many happy days were enjoyed, are only the poet's licence, taken to give zest to his rhymes, and represent no shade of ill-feeling or complaint.

The verses were read by the author, Kenmure Maitland, at the house-heating of our new Sabinum.

The next song, "The Wail of a Nestlin'," bears, it will be seen, on the same sorrowful subject.

The Old Nest and The New.

P.—— P.——, of F.——,
   By "Selkirk's souters" swore,
.That the Edinburgh Angling Club
   Should hold "the Nest" no more.
By the souters nine he swore it,
   And legal notice sent,
That the Club should their possession cede,
   And pay their last term's rent.

Forth went the fatal fiat
  To the Captain of the Club,
And fierce and fell the Members' rage
  At this unkindly rub !

A general meeting straight was called
  In horror and dismay,
And first with P.—— P.——
  They tried to fleech and pray.
They offered him the right to fish
  On each alternate day—
Yea, all the rights of membership,
  If he would let them stay ;
But obstinately he refused
  To compromise or yield—
The Club *must* leave the Robin's Nest,
  And seek some other field.

Then out spoke David Simson,
  Nathaniel without guile,
Though fiercely gleamed his eye that day,
  His lips forgot to smile.
" Ah.! woe is me !   This cruel blow
  Must strike our hearts full sore ;
God wot, we have been happy here
  These twenty years and more.
Dear as this place is to you all,
  'Tis thrice as dear to me,
For wife, and home, and happiness,
  I've found them here all three ;

But may the chiel who calls it his,
    And makes us feel his power,
Ne'er taste those joys we can't forget
    In this our parting hour."

Then up rose George Ximenes next,
    Who builds the mighty ships,
" Would I had P.—— P.——,"
    Quoth he, " within my grips ;
But let us wash our hands of him,
    Nor cry o'er milk that's spilled ;
We'll raise a new Nest for ourselves,
    E'en though we have to build.
" By fair Tweedside are other lairds
    Who'll welcome us with glee,
The Lairds of Yair or Ashiestiel,
    Or eke of Torwoodlee.
And other streams and pools there are,
    And many a salmon cast,
Beyond the banks of Fernielee,
    With all its glories past.
Then let us a committee name,
    A council say of three,
With powers full, to choose a site
    Where our new home shall be."

Then straightway took the council up
    Their duties, full of zeal,
And chose a site at Caddonlee,
    That faces Ashiestiel.

The ground is leased from Torwoodlee,
　　To whom our thanks are due
(And when our lease is out, we trust
　　He will the same renew).
And now, as if by magic raised,
　　Upon that fair hillside
Our new house stands, all furnishèd,
　　Our comfort and our pride.

Yet still, though here, perhaps, we find
　　More room, more light and air,
Some fond regrets *will* touch our hearts
　　For the dear old Nest at Yair.
And though friend Robert and his wife
　　Dwell with us as of yore,
And the same fair Grace[1] doth minister,
　　Who ministered before,
Yet something of the homeliness
　　Of our old home we miss,
And we of it think tenderly
　　In such an hour as this ;

The sweet romance that hedged it in
　　So cosily all round,
The murmur of the rushing Cauld,
　　With its soothing, silver sound ;
The little Gothic windows,
　　The roses on the wall,

---

[1] Our keeper's daughter, who has long attended to the domestic arrangements of the cottage.

The glory of the rustic porch—
    That brightest gem of all !

What ! tho' the tall men knocked their heads,
    And found the beds full short,
Why, e'en discomforts such as these
    Were but a theme for sport ;
And many a merry night, spent there,
    With tale, and song, and jest,
Will long live in the memory
    Of member, and of guest.

New fishings we've secured, on lease,
    As good as those we lose,
From Caddon Foot to Betty's Pool,
    We've all the way to choose.
Yet memory often, in our dreams,
    By day as well as night,
Each stretch of water, down below,
    Will paint in colours bright ;

From where, at foot of Neidpath Fell,
    Tweed sweeps o'er rocky bed
(The salmon fisher wading *there*
    Must step with cautious tread).
From Neidpath Foot it hurries down,
    With many a rippling gleam,
Till the shadows from the twin ash trees
    Fall o'er the Bogle stream ;
And then its murmur hushes,
    As, deepening and slow,

Beneath the alder bushes there,
    It steals with silent flow.

Of all the bends on silver Tweed
    Where is there one so fair,
As that in front of Fernielee,
    The famed 'Boat-pool of Yair ?
The fringing trees droop tenderly
    From banks of sward all green,
And in the waters, passing by,
    Their mirror'd grace is seen ;
And when the summer zephyrs blow,
And swing the branches hanging low,
    Soft kisses pass between.

Go view that scene in month of June
    When the hawthorn is in flower,
And the flakes of pure white blossom fall
    Like snow in summer shower,
The sweetness of that fairy spot
    Sinks to the inmost soul;
Here one could dream his life away,
    Nor seek for farther goal.

O'er the Yair Cauld the river breaks,
    All sparkling in the sun,
Rejoicing, like a child at play,
    In rapid race to run.
Then, stilled once more, as round it sweeps
    By the depths of Elm-Weil,

Where many a goodly fish has died
  To music of the reel.

How fair the view from the old bridge,
  By moonlight's silver sheen !
Right merrily the waters dance
  Through the Yair Trows, I ween.
Then, down across the Brander,
  The stream goes rushing fast,
Till Burnet's Cairn, the Rac-Lees,
  And Russel's Rock are past.

Then the Rae-Weil, lov'd haunt of kelts,
  With its fatal standing stone,
Where many a hook and line are lost,
  By tyro rashly thrown.
And then, the famous spawning bed,
  And the Island down below,
And " Arris' Putt," our final cast,
  Where we turn and homeward go.

So now, that debt to memory paid,
  And softly dropt the tear
Of fond regret o'er Fernielee,
  Let us look round us here.
Where we but found a wilderness
  Bleak on the hill-side's brow,
Our clustering trees take kindly root,
  And a garden bloometh now ;

And when, at eve, our gables
  Are seen against the sky,

U

And the upward curling smoke that speaks
   Of food, and stockings dry—
Then as our hungry fishers
   Arrive with weary pace,
They find our lines have fallen
   Truly in a pleasant place.

And now, a meed of grateful thanks
   Is due to all who've lent
Their kindly aid to make this place
   A palace of content.
To the council who approved the plans
   And saw them carried out,
Who planted all the grounds, and made
   The garden round about ;

And thanks to him who gave the trees
   That make so fair a show,
His memory will live green with us,
   As year by year they grow ;
To those who gave the shrubs and flowers,
   And to the members all
Who've helped to decorate our home,
   In garden and in hall.

And here's to our good President,
   The founder of this feast,
May his shadow ne'er grow less, but be
   From year to year increased !
And yet, another bumper still
   We'll drink before we part,

To one who our best interests
  Has ever at his heart—

Our Secretary Stewart—
  The king of anglers he,
Who floored Sir Cholmondely Pennell
  The " Typical Cockney."
So long as parr shall turn to smolt,
  And hasten to the sea,
So long as trout our waters haunt,
  His name shall honoured be.

Lastly, we'll drink our noble selves,
  And here, where now we dine,
May we be happy, as we've been
  In the days of auld langsyne !

The Wail of a Nestlin'.

AIR—" *The Flowers o' the Forest.*"

AULD Fernielee's tower,
  Wi' its ivy busked owre,
Sighed ance to the sang o' a leddy sae braw,
  Through my brain it keeps ringin',
  Till I'm greetin not singin',
For the Flowers o' *oor* Forest are a' wede awa' !

  Nae mair in the gloamin'
  Shall we come frae our roamin',
Ilka chiel wi' his Saumon, or maybe wi' twa ;
  A' the kelpies are sobbin',
  And our auld kimmer Robin,
Nae baccy, his fob in, can find for a " blaw."

  Ilka nicht like a rosy
  Bit gem, or a posy,
Our curtain, sae cosy, wad through the mirk glint ;
  But noo we are Nestless,
  Our beds are a' guestless,
Our hearts wae an' restless, for a' we hae tint.

  I canna get owre it—
  Ilka bonnie bricht flow'ret
Our Robin has tended in sunshine and snaw,
  Lies droopin' and deein' ;
  Tears start my sad e'e in,
For the flowers o' *oor* Forest are a' wede awa' !

Our Border Peel.

Air—" *Gae fetch to me a pint o' wine.*"

WHERE Elibank wi' men in steel
  Rade ower the hill—his spurs a' gory—
Where 'yont the Tweed a wizard sat,
  And wove the spells o' Border story,
A Nest we ken o' honest men,
  Wha love to bide where streams are singin',
And coont *ae* day, by pool and brae,
  Worth ten where city chimes are ringin';
      We'll cast the flee until we dee,
        We'll troll wi' glee a blithesome chorus;
      Till, in our Peel by Ashiestiel,
        Auld Daddie Care shall flee before us.

Bauld Rovers we frae Caddonlee !
  The Border streams we haunt and harry ;
Frae putt and weil we heap the creel,
  And deep into the dusk we tarry.
And, as we weigh our gallant prey,
  We drink a stoup to freends that angle—
Blithe be their day by pool and brae,
  But deil tak' a' that rail and wrangle !

      (CHORUS.)

The wind may blaw, the brown leaf fa',
   The wintry flaw may chill and chide us ;
We canna' mourn for simmer dead,
   While stout October lives beside us.
What care we, though the berry's red
   On briers, where late the rose was bloomin',
For aye the spate comes doon the glen,
   And up the siller fish come soomin'!

      (CHORUS.)

The years that pass wi' silent wing,
   May sprinkle snaw on beard and tresses—
May dim the e'e and fade the lip
   That wooed us to its saft caresses ;
But here we flout the touch o' Time ;
   Nae heart dare keep a room for sorrow ;
We fished yestreen !   We've fished to-day !
   And, by the rod ! we'll fish to-morrow !

      (CHORUS, *ad libitum.*)

The Bonny Trout.

Our album here, tells mony a queer
    Exploit o' saumon catchin',
Though strange it seem, I hae a theme,
    An' ane that there's nae matchin'.
Beyond a doot the bonny trout
    Are worthy o' the praisin',
Sae be it mine to write a line,
    To some folk maist amazin'.

Gie me a day, in lightsome May,
    When trout are in their prime,
An' ye may hae the brawest day
    In saumon fishin' time.
Let ithers sigh to cast their fly
    For Kipper, Baggit, Kelt,
Gie me the joy without alloy,
    That's only to be felt

When carefully ye cast your flee
    On some fine trouting stream,
And see them rise to tak' the flies,
    Their sides like siller's gleam.
The "Tid" is on, see yon big one,
    Cast soft above him there ;
The line is stent, the rod is bent,
    You've got him!—hae a care !

Wi' first a splash, and then a dash
    He goes wi' lichtnin' speed,

Then up he springs as if he'd wings,—
   O' losing him tak' heed.
At last he's done, the battle's won,
   He's safely in your creel;
Noo till't again, ye little ken
   What next may birl your reel.

Sae on ye go, and still ye throw
   Right carefully yer flies,
And aye look out to hook a trout
   Whaure'er ye see ane rise.
The western sun shows day is done,
   And calmly sinks to rest;
Sae hame ye gang, but wi' a pang,
   Ee'n though its tae the "*Nest.*"

And then ye tell, hoo it befell
   Ye lost a twa three pounder,
But when in bed ye lay your head
   Yer sleep's nae less the sounder.
And should you dream, be trout the theme
   That skelters through ye'r mind;
Nae better sport o' ony sort
   I'd wish for human kind!

[ANOTHER HAND APPENDS IN THE ALBUM *his* EXPERIENCE
  OF TWEED TROUT FISHING.]—

Folks write about the bonny trout,
   But I just mean to say,
He's easier far to rhyme about
   Than what he is to slay.

𝔄 𝔜oung 𝔐ember's 𝔉irst 𝔗rial of the 𝔗weed.

TUNE—"*For a' that, an' a' that.*"

I TOOK the train ae nicht in June,
　To gie the "Nest" a ca', man,
And Robert met me, and, says he,
　"They're takin'! Come awa', man."
My rod's soon up, the water's reached,
　We started at the wa', man,

It looked as like a fishin' nicht
  As fisher ever saw, man.
    But O man, and O man,
      New flees were tried and a', man,
     The trouts o' Tweed, say what ye will,
      Are the dourest trouts of a', man !

My flees fell down the water on
  As licht as flakes o' snaw, man,
But though I fished richt carefullie
  The deil a fin I saw, man !
The nicht grew dark, still I fished on
  In hopes o' ane or twa, man,
But though my flees were Robert's choice,
  The deil a fin I saw, man !
    (CHORUS.)

Though late the nicht, when we cam' hame,
  I took anither blaw, man,
For I had fished six weary hours,
  An' deil a fin I saw, man !
Auld Robert said, "They'll tak' the morn,
  But early at the da', man,"
Says I, then Robert, I'm your man,
  Be sure gie me a ca', man.
    (CHORUS.)

We started fresh, 'twas sharp at three,
  And fished richt on till twa, man ;
But though I tried baith worm and flee,
  The deil a fin I saw, man.

I tried my flask, nae change o' luck,
  And sine I tried a blaw, man ;
It wadna do, 'twas just the same,
  The deil a fin I saw, man !
      (CHORUS.)

I've fished wi' worm, I've fished wi' flee,
  Tried minnow, par, and a', man,
But the d—n—d trouts here never feed,
  They wadna tak' ava', man.
I've fished in lochs, in rivers too,
  In burns, baith big and sma', man,
But the Tweed's the dourest water yet,
  A fisher ever saw, man !
      (CHORUS.)

Still though the trouts are dour to tak',
  Now when the water's sma', man,
Auld Robert aye keeps tellin' me
  I shouldna gang awa' man,
But if the fates may have decreed
  Nae trouts I tak' awa', man,
My hooks, I'll swear, shall grip them yet
  When next I'm here awa', man !
      (CHORUS.)

The Pout Net.

THE "Pout Net" is not often seen in these days, and its use is not free from objection; but it seems to have been tried by some members, of loose principles, on the occasion of a heavy flood in April 1876, when a young hand, who was aiding and abetting, regardless of the sacred principle of "honour among thieves," disappeared by the evening train with all the proceeds of the "pout."

The Pout Net.

AIR—" *Tak yer auld cloak aboot ye.*"

'TWAS April, an' the Tweed cam' doon,
    An' snaw was seen on ilka hill,
An' floods o' rain an' blasts o' win'
    Were threatenin' a' oor lambs to kill ;
Whan Robert says, " O' a' the days
    That Tweed in spate ye e'er could see,
On this ane gin ye'd catch a troot,
    Tak' the auld pout net oot wi' ye.

" Oor pout net is a guid auld net,
    An' mony a guid troot has she taen ;
An' whiles although she hankit fast,
    She aye got rid o' thorn or stane ;
An' noo that Tweed's sae big an' brown,
    An' lads frae Embro' twa or three
Hae wandered oot to catch a troot,
    Tak' the auld pout net oot wi' ye."

Nae doot oor net's a guid auld net,
    Says Willie Menzies, but I'm sure,
Tweed's owre clear yet, a troot to get,
    Though ye suld fish for twenty year.

But Usher pit his troosers on,
   An' doon the Haugh tae Tweed went he ;
An' soon's he spied it, loud he sang,
   Bring the auld pout net doon wi' ye.

They heaved the pout net aue an' a',
   An whiles got troot an' whiles got nane,
When Robert gied the net awa'
   Tae Willie, wha tae throw't was fain.
He gripp'd the hawnle o' the net,
   An' raised it in the lift fu' hie,
Syne dived it down intil the flood,
   An' the auld pout net brak' did he.

I wat its guid lang twenty year
   An' mair, sin' Robert did begiu
Tae steek a hawnle till that net,
   An' ca'ed a nail tae keep it in.
Noo by that weary nail it's brak',
   But that sport suldna ended be,
He whittled it, and pit it back,
   Sayin', "Tak' the auld net noo wi' ye."

They hadna gaen aboon a mile,
   Or, at the outside, maybe twa,
When in the net ilk ane did get
   Mair trout than he was fit to draw.
The wind blew cauld, the rain cam' doon,
   Wi' driftin' weet ye scarce could see,
But still they toomed their flasks, an' cried,
   Tak' the auld pout net oot wi' ye.

Ilka man kens whan to lauch,
  An' ilk ane kens whan tae look skeered ;
Whan they cam hame, whaur a' the trout
  Had gane, sma' wonder that they speired.
For owre the Hill, whan it was mirk,
  That nicht folk saw a vision flee,
That, creel in han', skrieghed as it ran,
  Tak' the auld pout net oot wi' ye !

The Saumon v. the Trout.

Air—"*Fie, let's awa to the bridal.*"

THERE'S some folk like fishin' for Saumon,
　An' gran' sport it's for them, nae doot,
But though its' excitin' an' a', man,
　Commen' me to fishin' for Troot.
There's bottom, an' what's ca'ed float, fishin',
　Sea fishin', wi' bits o' red cloot,
An' fishin', beside stagnant water,
　But what's that tae fishin' for Troot !
　　　Then though some like fishin' for Saumon,
　　　　An' gran' sport it's for them, nae doot ;
　　　Yet, wi' its excitement an' a', man,
　　　　Commen' me to fishin' for Troot !

They stan' a' the day in the water,
　That's whiles higher up than their doup,
An' fecht wi' deep holes, an' wi' currents,
　An' aiblins ower muckle stanes coup.
Lang casts agin' sun, win', an' weather,
　Gar scaudin' tears rin doon their cheeks ;
Wi' wadin' an' sweatin' they're drookit,
　Baith outside an' inside their breeks.
　　　　(CHORUS.)

They tell ye the water's in order,
　A spate's brocht them a' they could wish,
Wi' Doctor, or Blucher, or Fraser,
　Ye're certain tae capture a fish.
But, Rampy, the Peel, or the Gullets,
　Ye'll fish an' nae Saumon get oot,

Whereas, ye're aye sure o' a nibble
　Whane'er ye gang fishin' for Troot.
　　　(CHORUS.)

That Saumon's the king o' the water
　There's naebody wants tae dispute;
But though they be reckoned a sma' fish,
　There's nane tries yer skill like a Troot.
Oh! leeze me an hour in the water,
　A ten-foot bit rod in my han',
Tae find ilka cast something tuggin',
　I think that there's naething sae gran'!
　　　(CHORUS.)

The fishin' for Saumon's a maitter
　Conneckit wi' grandeur an' storm;
Wi' forest, an' mountain, an' torrent,
　An' a'thing that's awsome in form;
But natur', in time o' Troot fishin',
　In saftness and beauty's decked oot;
Green fields, leafy woods, an' bricht blossoms,
　Surround ye, whan fishin' for Troot.
　　　(CHORUS.)

Some sports bring folk hame to their denner
　Wi' stamacks a sardine may suit,
Red herrin', or maybe a Finnan;
　But gie me a dishfu' o' Troot.
Then wi' a bit pockfu' o' worms,
　Or book fu' o' flees, we'll gang oot,
An' blithely we'll into the water,
　An' bring hame a basket o' Troot!
　　　(CHORUS.)

Y

Good Night.

'Tis time to part; the fleeting hours
  Too soon have sped their course along;
Yet surely we have tipped their wings
  With golden mirth and silv'ry song.
Old Time, upon his labouring course,
  Might pause to gaze on scenes so bright
And hours like these.   But, no, he's past,
  And we must part—Good night! Good night!

We'll meet again; you know the spot,
  Where rolls the river broad and fair,
Where peeps the modest violet,
  And hawthorn blossoms scent the air.
Again with song and mirth we'll crown
  Our long, long days of calm delight;
But now, alas! 'tis time to part,
  To each and all—Good night! Good night!

Early Days.

AMONG the many benefits which a diligent perusal of the preceding pages will have conferred upon the fortunate possessor of the volume, is the knowledge he will have obtained of some parts of the history of the EDINBURGH ANGLING CLUB. If, as ought to be the case, he be possessed of an inquiring mind, he will certainly desire to have further information upon this point, and ask where and how it can be got; and with an eye to this natural and proper inquiry, some attempt has been made to obtain the necessary material.

Like many other old and much loved institutions, the EDINBURGH ANGLING CLUB is not altogether clear as to its early career. Mist has gathered round its young days, when it was not the fashion to note everything with so much precision as now. Still, there are happily left to the Club two members—WILLIAM FORREST and ARTHUR PERIGAL—who were among its founders, and who are able to lift a corner of the veil that obscures its early history. It seems, then, that in 1847, several worthy men who "were thoroughly attached to, and conversant with, 'fishing with an angle,'" resolved to form themselves into a club, and to take a stretch of water on the Tweed, on which they might enjoy their favourite sport. At first they found shelter in a modest building known as "Betty's Cottage." It is still in existence, a pleasant one-floored cottage, within a mile of the new Nest. Some attempt seems to have been made to get a lease of the cottage and of Thornilee water, and such a lease was actually drafted. Difficulties arose, however. The Club fell for a brief time into the hands of the lawyers. Dim recollections exist of an "interdict," and of some other Court of Session proceedings. The result was, that the proposed arrangement fell through. Then, for the season of 1848, the Club had possession of Clovenfords House; and, after that, at the end of 1848 or the beginning of 1849, migrated to "The Nest," of which so many loving recollections are found in the songs.

The further career of the Club has been already described; and it only remains to add as perfect a list of the members from the commencement as can be obtained. Possibly two or three names may have been omitted, but the list, it is believed, is tolerably complete, and it is one upon which present and future members of the Club may look with much satisfaction and not a little pride.

List of Members

SINCE THE FORMATION OF THE CLUB IN 1847.

Elected.

1847.	WILLIAM FORREST,	.	.	.	Edinburgh.
	ARTHUR PERIGAL,	.	.	.	.	„
	ROBERT INNES,	.	.	.	.	„
	J. TROTTER,	.	.	.	.	„
	J. MARTIN,	.	.	.	.	„
	J. MILLER,	.	.	.	.	„
	— GELLATLY,	.	.	.	.	„
	JOSEPH LOWE,	.	.	.	.	„

Elected.

1847.	J. Walker,	.	. Edinburgh.
	Alexander Russel,		,,
	W. Miller,	.	,,
	David Wylie,	.	,,
	— Orrock of Orrock.		
	— Barton,		. Cascade.
	T. Scott,	.	. Edinburgh.
1848.	Charles Morton,		,,
	George Simson,	.	,,
	David Simson,	.	,,
	James Macdonald,		,,
	Robert Caunter,		,,
	John Gray,	.	,,
	Robert Gill,	.	. Galashiels.
	John Pringle,	.	. ,,
	Thomas Dunn,	.	. Edinburgh.
	John Dunn,	.	. Paisley.
1852.	George Menzies,	.	. Leith.
	George Stuart,	.	. Edinburgh.
	William Muir,	.	. Leith.
	E. Edmunds,	.	. Edinburgh.
	Dr Graham,	.	,,
	Charles M'Gibbon,	.	,,
	Sheriff Arkley,	.	,,
	John A. Macrae,		,,
	C. Robertson,	.	,,
	James W. Finlay,		,,
1856.	Alexander Ramsay,		,,
,,	Alexander Fraser,	.	,,
,,	R. B. Forsyth Brown,	.	,,
,,	Dr Brown,	.	,,
1857.	John Kennedy,	.	,,
,,	George Wood,	.	,,
,,	Dr Martin,	.	,,
1858.	George Webster,	.	,,
,,	Adam Morrison,		,,

Elected.

1858.	JAMES T. BLACK,	Edinburgh.
1860.	A. RUTHERFURD-CLARK,	,,
1861.	W. C. STEWART,	,,
,,	KENMURE MAITLAND,	,,
,,	Professor HENDERSON,	,,
,,	GEORGE DOVE,	,,
,,	ALEXANDER HOWE,	,,
1862.	THOMAS MENZIES,	,,
,,	LOCKHART THOMSON,	,,
1863.	Dr SKAE,	,,
1864.	GEORGE ROBERTSON,	,,
,,	W. S. HILL,	,,
1866.	JAMES COWAN,	,,
,,	WILLIAM HANDYSIDE,	,,
,,	JOHN KIDD,	Leith.
,,	JOHN M'KIE,	Glasgow.
,,	W. H. HAIG,	Fife.
,,	WILLIAM TOD,	Lasswade.
1867.	L. LA COUR,	Leith.
,,	J. STEEL,	Carlisle.
1868.	WILLIAM RUSSELL,	Leith.
,,	Dr W. F. COLLIER,	Edinburgh.
,,	WILLIAM J. MENZIES,	,,
,,	THOMAS AITKEN,	Leith.
,,	Dr A. DALZIEL,	Edinburgh.
,,	JAMES ROBERTSON,	,,
1870.	WILLIAM MENZIES,	,,
,,	THOMAS PHIPPS,	Trinity.
,,	J. CUNNINGHAM,	Liverpool.
,,	Dr STEVENSON MACADAM,	Edinburgh.
,,	J. R. PARK,	Leith.
,,	ROBERT C. TRAILL,	Edinburgh.
,,	SAMUEL D. DAVISON,	Leith.
,,	JOHN M. CRABBIE,	,,
1871.	ANDREW JAMES USHER,	Edinburgh.
1872.	ARCHIBALD F. SOMERVILLE,	,,

Elected.

1873.	ANDREW AITKEN,	Leith.
,,	Dr JAMES STRUTHERS,	,,
,,	A. W. HAMILTON,	. Row.
,,	JAMES LAW, .	. Edinburgh.
1874.	ANTHONY WATSON, .	. Leith.
1875.	WILLIAM MENZIES, Jun.,	. Newcastle.
,,	JOHN SMART, . .	. Edinburgh.
,,	SAMUEL L. MASON,	,,
1876.	Dr J. SMITH, .	,,
,,	ALEXANDER NIMMO,	. Falkirk.
1877.	JOHN W. YOUNG,	Edinburgh.
,,	J. S. FLEMING, .	,,
,,	JAMES SOMERVILLE,	,,
1878.	CHARLES A. COOPER,	,,
,,	ALEXANDER O. COWAN, .	,,

Honorary Members.

DAVID C. ALEXANDER, .	. Selkirk.
GEORGE OUTRAM,	. Glasgow.
Dr MACLAGAN, .	. Edinburgh.

THE MEMBERS AT THE CLOSE OF 1878 ARE—

1847.	ARTHUR PERIGAL, *Vice-President,*	. Edinburgh.
1848.	CHARLES MORTON, *President,* .	. ,,
1852.	GEORGE MENZIES,	. Leith.
1856.	ALEXANDER FRASER,	. Edinburgh.
1862.	THOMAS MENZIES,	,,
,,	JOHN KIDD, . .	. Leith.
,,	WILLIAM HANDYSIDE, . .	. Edinburgh.
1867.	L. LA COUR, . . .	. Leith.
1868.	THOMAS AITKEN, . . .	,,
1870.	WILLIAM MENZIES, *Secretary and Treasurer,*	Edinburgh.

Elected.

1870.	Thomas Phipps, .	. Trinity.
,,	Dr Stevenson Macadam,	. Edinburgh.
.,	Robert C. Traill,	,,
,,	Samuel D. Davison,	. Leith.
1871.	Andrew James Usher, .	. Edinburgh.
1872.	Archibald F. Somerville,	,,
1873.	Andrew Aitken,	. Leith.
,,	A. W. Hamilton,	. Row.
,,	James Law,	. Edinburgh.
1874.	Anthony Watson,	. Leith.
1875.	William Menzies, Jun.,	. Newcastle.
,,	John Smart,	. Edinburgh.
,,	Samuel L. Mason,	,,
1876.	Dr J. Smith,	,,
,,	Alexander Nimmo,	. Falkirk.
1877.	John W. Young,	. Edinburgh.
,,	J. S. Fleming,	,,
,,	James Somerville,	,,
1878.	Charles A. Cooper,	,,
,,	Alexander O. Cowan, .	,,

Honorary Members.

| William Forrest, | . Edinburgh. |
| Dr Maclagan, . | ,, |

PRINTED BY NEILL AND COMPANY, EDINBURGH.

www.ingramcontent.com/pod-product-compliance
Lightning Source LLC
Chambersburg PA
CBHW030538040726
47497CB00008B/2497